Ghost Twins

4

The Missing Moose Mystery

Dian Curtis Regan

Also in the Ghost Twins series

Have you read?
The Mystery at Kickingbird Lake
The Mystery of One Wish Pond
The Mystery on Walrus Mountain

Look out for:
The Mystery of the Disappearing Dogs
The Haunted Campground Mystery

JUNIPER DAILY NEWS

New Autumn Fashions Inside!

Twins Involved in Boating Mishap

Robert Adam Zuffel and his twin sister, Rebeka Allison, seem to be victims of a boating accident at Kickingbird Lake. Their dog, Thatch, disappeared with them. Family members say that the twins had gone hiking on Mystery Island and were probably returning when yesterday's windstorm blew up.

Their overturned canoe was floating in the water off Mystery Island. A party of family members searched the lake and the surrounding area, and no trace of the twins or their dog was found.

Today's Highlights

President Roosevelt Welcomes Cary Grant to White House　pg.2

Zoot Suits All the Rage　pg.3

Movie Review: *Bambi*　pg.5

Local Student Wins Award for Model of All 48 States　pg.6

To Cindy Knox, for obvious reasons

Scholastic Children's Books,
Commonwealth House, 1-19 New Oxford Street,
London WC1A 1NU, UK
a division of Scholastic Ltd
London ~ New York ~ Toronto ~ Sydney ~ Auckland

First published in the US by Scholastic Inc., 1995
Published in the UK by Scholastic Ltd, 1996

Copyright © Dian Curtis Regan, 1995

ISBN 0 590 13596 1

Typeset by TW Typesetting, Midsomer Norton, Avon
Printed by Cox & Wyman Ltd, Reading, Berks.

10 9 8 7 6 5 4 3 2 1

Contents

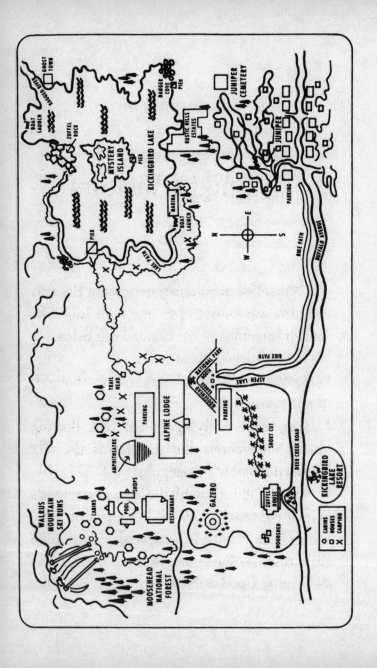

Chapter 1
Midnight Visitors

The sound of hammering brought Beka off the top bunk bed in one swift leap. She landed smoothly on the braided rug below.

Darkness filled the attic.

It's the middle of the night, she thought. *What's going on?*

Beka had been lying on her bed, floating through memories and daydreams the way ghosts do instead of sleeping.

Now she stole through the blackness towards one of the front windows. Pinpoints of light, shining from outside, reflected off the high attic beams. The squiggly lines appeared to be staging a sword fight.

"Hi," came a voice from the shadowed window seat.

Beka jumped.

Her twin brother, Robbie, was already there, watching the scene below. Their dog, Thatch, was there, too; half on, half off the window seat, panting on the glass. He seemed eager to figure out what was going on.

Gingerly, Beka peeked out the window. Ever since she'd heard talk of "wispy ghost faces" staring out of the attic windows of the "old Zuffel house", she'd been self-conscious about gazing out of the windows.

Below, parked in the centre of the front drive that curved from Deer Creek Road to the steps of the veranda, was a truck. On its door, the letters *KLR*, for Kickingbird Lake Resort, caught the torches' beams.

"Why are Mr Tavolott's workers here in the middle of the night?" Beka asked, confused. "And what are they building?"

"As far as I can tell," her brother answered, "they're building a ramp on to one side of the veranda steps."

"A ramp? What for?"

As if to answer her question, headlights turned up the drive, throwing beams across the front of the house. A resort van parked behind the truck. A man wearing a cowboy hat got out.

"It's Mr Tavolott himself," Robbie said. "Boy, this *must* be important for the owner of the resort to be out here in the middle of the night."

A girl climbed out of the passenger seat, slowly, as if awakened in the middle of a dream for a secret journey. Her long dark hair was tousled, and she wore a heavy jacket even though spring was in the air.

Following Mr Tavolott to the veranda, she waited while he inspected the ramp. Then he waved the workers away. They climbed into their truck and headed down the drive.

Mr Tavolott hurried up the steps. The twins could hear him opening the door. Lights came on, reflecting off the front railing.

Returning to the van, Mr Tavolott opened the back and pulled out travelling bags of various sizes, plus a huge steamer trunk. The girl helped him carry the trunk and bags inside. The last thing he carried in appeared to be a birdcage.

Next, Mr Tavolott helped the girl unfold some kind of metal contraption.

"Is it a wheelchair?" Robbie asked.

"Looks like it." Beka remembered the wheelchair President Roosevelt sat in. (*Used to sit in*, her memory corrected. Sometimes the passage of fifty years seemed like only a few. At least ten presidents must have taken Roosevelt's place by now.)

Mr Tavolott and the girl helped an elderly woman from the van.

"I can't see much from here," Beka said. "Let's go downstairs."

She could tell by Thatch's eager whining that he was more than ready.

They hurried down the attic steps, around the second-floor landing, then down the polished wooden staircase to the entry hall.

Mr Tavolott pushed the wheelchair up the ramp while the girl held the front door open.

In the light, Beka could see the colour of the girl's hair. Orangey-red. The colour *she'd* always wished for. Lucky girl. She was the same height as Beka, and had just as many freckles sprinkled across her face.

Mr Tavolott had difficulty getting the wheelchair to roll across the threshold. "I'll have my workers come back and install a smooth metal plate here so the wheels will roll right over."

"No need," the woman said. "I don't plan to leave the house."

Beka stared at her as she rose from the chair and reached for the young girl's arm.

The woman was striking. White hair framed a lightly wrinkled face. Dark glasses hid her eyes.

Why is she wearing dark glasses in the middle of the night? Beka wondered. *And why is she in a wheelchair if she can walk?*

"Can I help you to your room, Nell?" Mr Tavolott asked, removing his cowboy hat. "Or get you a snack? My staff stocked the cupboards with the food you requested."

"You're very kind," she replied. "But no. Jamie here will take good care of me. She always does."

Mr Tavolott patted the girl on the shoulder. "You're very lucky to have such a fine grand-daughter."

The girl – Jamie – ducked her head, embarrassed.

"I truly am," the woman said. "When her parents return from their year of teaching in Tokyo, I'm not sure I'll let them reclaim their daughter."

"Wow," Beka said. Tokyo sounded so far away.

Meanwhile, Thatch was busy checking out the midnight visitors. Especially the ones who'd arrived in the birdcage. A cloth covered the cage, but it sounded as if there was more than one bird.

Thatch padded back and forth, sniffing the strangers, luggage and cage. Finally his curiosity got the better of him. After nudging the cloth long enough, his ghost powers took over, and the cloth began to inch up.

Jamie noticed it at the same time as Beka. Giving a puzzled look, she straightened the cloth that had somehow moved on its own.

Thatch grumble-barked at her.

Robbie stepped around the steamer trunk to grab the dog's collar.

Beka snapped her fingers to distract the dog. "All we need is for Thatch to scare off our newest guests before they even get in the door."

Normally, Beka wouldn't have minded. She liked having the house to themselves. But there was something about this girl and her grandmother – stealing into the house in the middle of the night – that teased her curiosity. She wanted to know more about them.

The woman extended her hand. "Thank you, Charles, for helping us, and agreeing to keep our little secret."

Secret? Beka and Robbie exchanged glances. This was getting more interesting by the minute.

"Your identity is safe with me," Mr Tavolott said. "No one will know the world-famous artist, Nell Makanda, is right here in Kickingbird."

Beka gasped. "Nell Makanda? She was famous even before we became ghosts."

Thatch barked, as though he were impressed, too.

The woman sighed, sounding tired from her late-night journey. "Well, it's good to be home once more."

She placed a hand against her cheek. "I was so looking forward to seeing Juniper again; seeing how much it's changed since the last time I was here. But I guess the *seeing* part will have to wait."

That's when Beka realized that the world-famous artist was blind.

Chapter 2
We've Got Trouble

After Mr Tavolott left, Beka made Robbie stay in the hall while Jamie helped her grandmother to bed in the spacious master bedroom.

Beka wanted to help, too, since Jamie had to do all the seeing for her grandmother. She kept reminding herself that she couldn't.

But she *could* listen to their conversation.

From what Beka could figure out, the grandmother's blindness was temporary, caused by a recent stroke. She'd come here to recover because reporters were hounding her for interviews.

Doctor's orders were "peace and quiet". The

famous Nell Makanda was getting neither in her home studio. Hence the secret, middle-of-the-night trip to Kickingbird Lake Resort.

"Do you want to sleep in here?" Jamie offered after tucking her grandmother in. "In case you need me? I can bed down on the sofa."

"No, dear, I'm fine. Surely there are lots of bedrooms in this old house. Find yourself a nice one and settle in. We'll take a look in the morning and see where we've landed."

"OK, Gran." Jamie bent to kiss her cheek. "Are you cold? Or hungry?"

"You're worse than Bartholomew!" the woman snapped. "He worries over me more than Dr Tekoa."

Jamie laughed. "Bartholomew was pretty insulted when you told him he couldn't come with us."

"Humph. I need someone at home to field phone calls. That's his job; to take care of my business – not to mother me to death."

She fluffed her pillows, then took off the dark glasses, feeling for the nightstand before setting them down. "Phone calls," she scoffed. "The *Times*, BBC, *Independent*. Enough. I'm just a tired old artist who worked too hard and ignored her doctor."

"Mmm," Jamie answered, absently peeking under the cloth on the cage to make sure the birds were fine. She closed the shutters and turned out the light. "Remember, the more you rest, the sooner your sight will return to normal."

"Now *you* sound like Dr Tekoa," Gran grumbled. "Hush and go to bed."

Jamie stepped into the brightly lit hallway. "Good night," she whispered, shutting the door.

Beka slipped out before the door closed.

Jamie glanced at her watch. "Now that I'm wide-awake, I might as well have a look around."

"Great," Robbie said, joining them. "I'll give you a tour of the Zuffel house."

Jamie wandered into a small room between the kitchen and formal dining room, clicking on lights.

"This is the butler's pantry," Robbie explained, "where food used to be prepared before being served in the dining room."

"Only *we* never had a butler," Beka added.

Jamie examined the wooden cabinets with antique glass doors. "Cool," she said, turning the corner into the kitchen.

"This is the kitchen," Robbie told her.

Beka looked at him strangely. "I *think* she figured that out."

Flipping on the light, Jamie opened the refrigerator. "Skimmed milk, fat-free yoghurt, cottage cheese and bottled water. Good."

Thatch made a beeline towards the open refrigerator, practically climbing on to the lower shelf.

Beka pulled him away before the door went through him – or crunched him. Either could happen when it came to the ghost dog.

Checking cupboards, Jamie rattled off their contents as well: wheat bread, rye crackers and a cereal box labelled *MUESLI*. Beka wondered what muesli was.

Jamie helped herself to a few crackers.

"No thanks," Robbie said. "But it was kind of you to offer."

Beka giggled. Why was her brother acting so daft?

Jamie tried the phone Mr Tavolott's workers had brought over with the food. Next, she opened cabinet drawers.

One was filled with brochures about Kickingbird and the town of Juniper. She took a few, then wandered around the first floor, all the way back to the conservatory, which overlooked the back yard.

Robbie "explained" each room, as if Jamie needed his brilliant assistance.

Satisfied, Jamie returned to the entry hall, grabbed her travelling bag, and headed upstairs, turning off lights as she climbed.

At the top, she paused. "Checking out a strange house in the middle of the night is … is *spooky*," she said to no one in particular.

"Spooky?" Beka echoed. "What if I told you *ghosts* were following you?"

Jamie twirled to peer down the dark stairway, almost as if she'd heard Beka's words.

"Don't scare her!" Robbie snapped.

Beka ignored him. "What if I told you the house – and your bedroom – are haunted? By the ghost twins of Kickingbird Lake and their ghost dog."

Robbie frowned at her.

Jamie toured the upstairs rooms, stopping at the end of the landing to inspect the narrow staircase to the second floor.

"Out of bounds!" Beka yelped, rushing to block the girl's path. "The attic is ours."

"Bek, I *told* you not to scare her." Anger coloured Robbie's words.

She stared at her brother. What had got into him?

Jamie didn't know a ghost girl stood on the step above her, yet something made her flip off the attic light and hurry away.

"She's going to pick my old bedroom," Beka said. "I know she will."

"Leave her alone, Raz." Robbie used the nickname formed from their shared initials. "Let Jamie go to bed." He steered his sister and the dog up the attic stairs.

Beka watched her brother. Something odd was happening here. But what?

Whistling a nonsense tune, he wandered across the attic to one of the window seats and gazed out at the moon.

Beka climbed to the top bunk.

Then it hit her.

She'd seen her brother act this way before.

Fourth grade. Spring term. The day that new girl had joined their class. What was her name? Beka had forgotten.

Making room for Thatch, Beka rolled over to study her brother.

Same vacant expression. Same concern for the girl's feelings.

"Oh, boy," Beka mumbled into Thatch's ruffly fur. "We've got trouble."

Thatch's puppy eyes wrinkled, as if he were truly concerned.

Beka kissed his nose and sighed. "My poor brother has fallen in love."

Chapter 3
Spring Has Sprung

*T*he *End.*

Beka closed the book. It was "due" today at the Sugarberry Library in Juniper. The librarians never suspected that a ghost patron "borrowed" books, yet Beka always followed the library's rules, returning books promptly.

"Wow, this was an exciting story." Beka studied the cover. A princess, dressed in scarlet from veil to slipper, stole through a witch's forest with a tiny pet dragon as her only protection.

This morning when Beka started reading, the sun had barely lit the attic. Now it was high in the midday sky, yet she hadn't been able to put the book down until she had found out how the scarlet princess fared.

Robbie and Thatch had gone downstairs hours ago.

Beka remembered the midnight arrival of the Makandas. Stacking the library book with the others, she hurried downstairs.

The house was quiet; the kitchen empty.

Minutes passed before Beka found anyone. Finally the squeak of a rocking chair led her to the conservatory.

She hadn't thought about looking here. The unheated room was sealed off in winter. But this morning, it was warm and pleasant.

The room used to be the twins' summer playroom. The hardwood floor had survived lots of games and races. Walls on three sides came up to Beka's waist. From there to the high ceiling were windows.

One end of the room caught the morning light, the other, afternoon sunshine, making this the cheeriest room in the house.

That's where Beka found Jamie's grandmother, sitting in a spot of sun in a rocking chair, humming contentedly.

Jamie was nowhere in sight, but Robbie sat on a built-in bench along the west wall. The seat of the bench opened on hinges. The twins used to store their toys inside.

Thatch had found his own splash of sunshine. He lay on his back, paws spread wide, allowing the spring sun to warm his tummy.

Beka wished for her old Brownie camera to capture a picture of Thatch's silliness.

"What are you doing?" she asked Robbie. It looked like he and Gran were having a heart-to-heart talk, but Beka knew that wasn't possible.

"Well, somebody needs to keep an eye on her." He acted embarrassed at being caught *babysitting*. "I mean, she was trying to find her way through the house, and almost fell."

"Where's Jamie?"

"Grandma Nell!"

Beka twirled.

Jamie, still wearing pyjamas, rushed into the conservatory. Her sleep-tousled hair sparkled red-gold in the morning light.

Robbie came to life, sitting up straight and smoothing his own hair.

Beka groaned.

"Are you OK?" Jamie asked, sounding worried.

"Don't I look OK?" Gran retorted.

"I couldn't *find* you. In your room. In the kitchen or family room. It scared me." Jamie knelt by her grandmother's chair. "How'd you get in here by yourself?"

Gran acted as if sitting in the sunshine, rocking and humming, was the most natural activity in the world. "I woke up early and wanted to take a look around – so to speak."

She reached out a hand and waited for Jamie to grasp it.

"There," she said. "I like knowing where you are when I talk to you. Please dig my cane out of those travelling bags. Finding my way out here left me with a few bruises from bumping into things." She rubbed one leg, as if to prove her point.

"I'll get it right away," Jamie said while finger-combing her hair. "Have you eaten yet?"

"No. Making a pot of hot coffee is better left to someone who can see."

"Let me help you to the kitchen so we can eat breakfast — before it's time for lunch." Jamie took hold of her grandmother's arm.

"Wait, dear. This room gives me a marvellous feeling. Describe it."

Jamie gave Gran a brief description of her surroundings.

"Is there a table in here?"

"No."

"Well, this is where I want to eat breakfast every morning. Call Charles and ask him to send over a table."

"Fine," Jamie said. "Stay right where you are, and I'll bring breakfast to you."

"And bring Picasso and Dalí with you. They would like it in here."

"Picasso and Dalí?" Beka echoed.

Hurrying into the kitchen, Jamie put water on to heat for coffee, then prepared bowls of fruit, cereal and yoghurt. In place of a table, she borrowed straight-backed chairs from the dining room to set up breakfast.

Then she carried in the birdcage, placing it in a sunny corner.

Two canaries chirped their approval.

"Ah," Beka said. "Picasso and Dalí."

Jamie sat on the floor to eat.

"Yoghurt." Robbie pretended to choke. "Yuk."

Even Thatch raised his head to sniff at the breakfast, but stayed where he was. Yoghurt wasn't much of a doggie treat, either.

Gran sipped her coffee. "Did you find a nice bedroom?"

"Yes, on the second floor. From one window, I can see trees bursting with pink blossoms, and robins building a nest. Oh, Grandma Nell, it's beautiful."

Gran looked pleased. "You have an artist's eye, Miss Makanda. Most folks would look out of that same window and never notice the nest."

Jamie glanced across the back yard, as if it was her duty as a young artist to take in every view.

"Did you sleep well?" Gran asked.

Jamie held her cereal spoon in mid-air, thinking. "No. I guess that's why I didn't wake up early this morning."

She took a few quick bites. "After I went to bed, something woke me. It was almost as if a dog had jumped on to my bed to see who was sleeping there. Seemed as if he curled up near my feet and stayed the rest of the night."

She closed her eyes to remember. "I'm sure I only dreamed it, but it was so real, I had trouble falling back to sleep."

"Thatch!" Beka and Robbie chimed together.

Beka shook a finger at him. "Shame on you. I thought you were with *me* in the attic."

Robbie *tsked* at Thatch, who didn't know what the fuss was all about. Rolling to his feet, the dog padded towards Jamie, sniffing at her bowl of muesli. Uninterested, he lay down next to her.

Why does the thought of Thatch sleeping on Jamie's bed bother me? Beka was suddenly unable to watch her dog snuggling up to the girl.

Well, she told herself, *Thatch and I have important things to do today, like books to return.* Thatch liked escorting her to the library. Probably because the smells there ranged from A to Z.

Ha! Beka laughed at her own joke.

"You'll never believe what I'm thinking," Gran said, interrupting Beka's daydream.

Setting her coffee cup on the chair, Gran stood, spreading her arms to take in the sunny room. "Coming back to Kickingbird was a wonderful idea. I feel stronger here. This room is healing. And," she added, facing Jamie's direction, "I feel like painting again."

Jamie gave a little gasp. "But Grandma Nell, you're—"

"Blind," the woman finished. "Not completely. I can still see images, although they're terribly blurred. But I do think my sight is getting better."

"But how—?"

"Dear, I've spent my whole life painting. I used to brag that I could paint with my eyes closed. Now's a chance to put my bragging to the test." Her wrinkles seemed to melt as she laughed.

Beka moved closer, enthralled with the way Gran's laughter brought this dusty old room to life. The way it made spring burst through the windows and blossom in the conservatory.

Even Robbie felt it. Coming off the bench, he joined them in the middle of the room – although his attention stayed fixed on Jamie.

"When you finish your breakfast," Gran continued, "help me set up my easel. May I use the art supplies we brought for you?"

"Of course."

"Will you go into Juniper and fetch more paint?"

Jamie seemed to be having difficulty taking in Gran's sudden excitement. "If you're sure…"

"I'm sure." Her voice was firm. "I never thought I'd feel like painting again for a long time. But I do. Pooh on Dr Tekoa's warnings and Bartholomew's worries."

Thatch sprang to his feet, prancing and barking.

Gran seemed to sense she was surrounded by fans, cheering her on. She shook a fist at fate. "By gum or by golly, this old blind artist wants to paint again – and paint, she will…"

Jamie looked shocked.

The twins applauded.

And Thatch gave Gran a six-bark salute.

Chapter 4
Ghost Escorts

An hour later, Jamie had showered, dressed, unpacked, and was on her way into Juniper with a shopping list from Gran.

Three invisible escorts hurried along beside her.

Beka balanced her library books against one hip, and breathed in the scent of blooming apple trees. Something about spring's arrival in Kickingbird was an event she always looked forward to.

One minute, the quiet cold of winter ruled. The next, April exploded on to the calendar, chasing winter away for another half-year.

Thatch was well aware of the sights and

smells of the season. Flocks of birds returned to the area with fanfare equal to the Fourth of July parade.

Beka watched the dog race ahead on the path, stopping to sniff each walker and biker – and those people who ran up and down the path for no reason that she could see.

Satisfied, Thatch dashed back for a quick pat from one of the twins before flying in the other direction to see who lagged behind.

Jamie stopped in the centre of town to study the map. "That's the town square," she said, peering at a large block of concrete stair-stepping up to an empty platform.

"Wait a minute." Jamie looked at a picture of "old Juniper" on the back of the brochure. "There's supposed to be a moose at the top of those steps. A bronze, life-size moose, in honour of Moosehead Forest."

"It's gone," Robbie told her. "Morty's been gone for years and years. Somebody stole him."

"I wonder what happened?" Jamie mumbled.

"Robbie just told you," Beka teased. "Pay attention."

Jamie shrugged, squinting at the map again. "Kickingbird Art and Office Supplies should be straight ahead."

"Follow us," Robbie said, taking the lead.

As they passed the library, Beka paused. "Let's drop off my books," she suggested, "and catch up with Jamie at the art supply shop."

"Umm." Robbie tried to kick a rock. Of course, it didn't move. "You go ahead. I'll stay with Jamie."

Jealousy twinged Beka's feelings. Last night, her dog had deserted her for Jamie, and now her brother was. "Why?" she asked.

"She might need help."

"And how do you plan to help her?"

Robbie didn't have an answer.

"Brothers," Beka groaned. "See you later."

She hurried up the library's high stone steps. Thatch bounded up behind her.

They waited by the double oak doors until somebody came along to open them. Beka watched Jamie continue down the street, a see-through boy tailing along at her side.

The sight was amusing, but Beka didn't smile. Instead, she rubbed Thatch's scruffy neck. At least *he* stayed with her this time.

A man finally breezed past and entered the library. She and Thatch slipped inside before the door closed.

Beka piled her books on the RETURN shelf. When she was sure no one was watching, she let go of the stack. The books sparked purple, making quick snapping sounds. Now she knew the books were visible in the "real world".

"Hi, Stan," she said, greeting the librarian, who was there almost every time she visited.

"Where did *those* come from?" he mumbled, reaching to check in the books that had suddenly appeared on the counter.

"From me," she grinned. Turning, she wandered between tall bookshelves, taking in the smell of dust and leather. The library was one of her favourite places in the whole world – next to Kickingbird Lake, the gazebo in her back yard, and the attic. She could *live* in the library and be perfectly happy.

Heading for the back stairway, she passed the library's brand-new addition — a community room. The large area was used for exhibits and receptions. The city of Juniper was presently sponsoring a contest to name the room.

Beka hurried up the wide stairway to the first floor. That's where *her* kind of books could be found. She read almost everything: mysteries, suspense, humour, biographies, sports, science fiction.

But not cookbooks. Boy, were they boring.

Thatch wandered off.

Beka's first thought was to catch the dog and keep him by her side, yet finding more books by the *Scarlet Princess* author shouldn't take long.

She soon found a whole shelf of them, but five was all she could comfortably carry. For twenty minutes, she scanned covers and read cover-copy to narrow her choices. It was a tough decision.

Noises filtered into Beka's brain as she slowly selected her books.

Noises in a quiet library?

She raised her head to listen. Then panic struck.

Quiet library+Thatch on the loose=noises.

Whoops!

Beka tucked the books under one arm and flew down the steps.

Where *was* that dog?

Follow the noises, her mind told her.

They led her to the door of the community room. A sign on the door caught her eye.

"Oh, no!" Beka moaned. Why hadn't she taken time to read it before?

TODAY!
FIRST ANNUAL CAT SHOW
COME AND SEE JUNIPER'S FINEST FELINES!

Chapter 5
Scaredy-cats

Beka felt as if someone had thrown a bucket of iced water in her face.

The commotion inside the community room could only be caused by a dog. A ghost dog.

Yet Beka was helpless until someone came along and opened the door – which is how Thatch got in.

Seconds slid into minutes before the door burst open. A plump woman clutching a white Persian cat to her chest rushed right *through* Beka! She was mumbling, "Mummy will save her precious Petunia."

Beka dashed into the room before the door slammed.

Chaos ruled.

There they were: tiny cats, fat cats. White, orange, and black cats.

Calicos, Persians, kittens and alley cats.

Those in cages cowered and clung. Yowling pierced the air.

Those *outside* cages took refuge on high shelves and under cloth-draped tables.

Owners flew about in tizzies, calming pets and coaxing them into cages.

Judges huddled in the middle of the room, speaking in frantic voices. "What happened?" they kept asking.

What a bunch of scaredy-cats. Beka imagined tomorrow's headline in the *Juniper Daily News*: FELINES FREAK FOR UNKNOWN REASON!

Thatch was beside himself. He streaked around the room, scrambling here to nip a puffy tail. Scrambling there to terrorize a caged cat, or bark another kitten up the curtains.

Of course, the cats couldn't *see* the ghost dog. But they knew he was there. *Boy* did they know he was there.

"Thatch!" Beka screamed.

Hearing his mistress, he galloped towards Beka, tongue out, panting. Jumping up on her, he seemed to say, "Look what I did! Isn't this fun?"

Beka was not amused.

"Time to go, troublemaker." Taking firm hold of his collar, she half-led, half-pulled him towards the door, which was now swinging open and closed as people fled with their cats – as soon as they caught them.

Thatch pulled against Beka's grasp, but no way was she letting go of his collar.

Rushing through the library, she passed the checkout desk, and bobbed her head at Stan. "I'll bring the books back next week," she hollered, hurrying out the door behind the next patron. "Sorry we ruined the cat show."

For once she wished her message would break through, loud and clear.

By the time Beka arrived at the art supply shop, Jamie and Robbie were nowhere in sight.

"They went home without us," Beka told

Thatch. "Thanks to you and the scarlet princess." She felt guilty about her dog's bad behaviour, but the memory of the "Cat Show Caper" made her laugh.

Ghost dogs were definitely entertaining.

At home, Beka was struck by a thought. Everyone was *inside*. She and Thatch were *outside*.

Making her way around the house, she climbed the steps of the veranda and peered through the conservatory windows.

There was Gran, waiting, while Jamie set up an easel. Large canvas panels leaned against the far wall, waiting to be painted.

Beka tapped the glass, catching Robbie's attention.

He motioned to her, but she didn't know what he was trying to say.

He was probably telling her to *smoosh*, which was the only way to get inside when doors were closed. *Smooshing* wasn't her favourite thing to do, and the headache it caused was a bother. Who *wouldn't* have a headache after dissolving their body and bringing it back together again?

Suddenly Jamie rushed from the room. In a few seconds, she returned, guiding two men carrying a long table.

Beka cupped her hands around her eyes for a better look. It was Mr Tavolott and his son, Michael, who wore a cowboy hat like his father.

Robbie was practically doing a dance now, trying to tell her something. Then Thatch appeared next to him.

How did the dog get inside? Had he *smooshed* without her?

As the men turned to leave, Beka got the point. They were carrying in furniture, which meant the front door was propped open. Dashing around the house, she breezed inside, pleased to be saved from *smooshing*.

Mr Tavolott set the steamer trunk full of art supplies within easy reach for Gran. Next he helped Jamie loosen lids. The scent of turpentine and linseed oil floated through the air.

"I was so pleased when you called," he told Gran. "Just think." He nudged his son.

"Juniper's own artist is going to paint right here in my house."

"It's *our* house," Beka reminded him.

Gran gave orders about where to place everything. Michael spread drop cloths on the floor to protect it from paint splatters. Jamie fetched a smock and helped Gran slip it on over her clothes.

"Remember, Charles," Gran said, "this studio is our little secret."

"Of course. That's why I'm personally delivering the furniture you requested."

"So the only ones who know Nell Makanda is here are you and Michael," Gran stated. "Is that correct?"

"Yes, ma'am," Mr Tavolott answered. "Unless the canaries squealed."

That made Beka laugh.

Thatch reared up on his hind legs, placing his front paws on Mr Tavolott's stomach for attention.

"Thatch, get down," Robbie ordered.

Mr Tavolott shivered, even though sunshine heated the room. "Is this room warm enough?" he asked. "I can deliver an electric heater."

Beka and Robbie exchanged grins. They knew Thatch's closeness had given Mr Tavolott the sudden chill.

"I'm fine," Gran said, running her hands across the rough surface of the canvas, as if feeling the scene taking shape in her mind. "And I'm eager to get started. But I *don't* need an audience."

Mr Tavolott touched two fingers to his hat. "We're off," he said. "And our lips are sealed. Just shout if you need me."

Gran didn't answer. She was already squeezing paint from tubes on to her palette.

"That's the burnt sienna," Jamie said, waving goodbye to the Tavolotts.

"I know, dear. If you lined the tubes up in the order I requested, then the colour I've chosen *should* be burnt sienna."

"Wow," Beka said. "She really *is* going to paint without seeing."

Robbie didn't answer. He was too busy staring at Jamie.

"Do you need anything else?" Jamie asked.

Gran raised her head, as if surprised anyone was still here. "Oh, child, forgive me. This is your spring holiday. You don't need to baby-sit me. Go outside and enjoy yourself. Why don't you hike up to the lake?"

"I'd love to go exploring," Jamie exclaimed, then hesitated. "As long as you're sure you won't be needing me."

"Put a two-inch red sable in your ol' grandmother's hand and she'll be in painter's heaven."

Jamie sorted through brushes, handing the requested one to her grandmother.

"Now get out of here, and go have fun."

The girl didn't need a second invitation. In a flash, she was out the door, the twins and Thatch close behind.

Chapter 6
The Gooseberry

"This is the short cut," Robbie said, leading the group through a grove of sand plums. "It cuts through these trees from the back yard to the road so you don't have to go around the long way."

"I'm sure she cares." Beka played chase along the path with Thatch. She always tried her best to beat him, but never could.

"In the old days," Robbie continued, "we used to cut across the hills to Kickingbird Lake, and come out near the marina. But now, it's easier to go straight to the ranger station in Moosehead and follow the footpaths."

"I'm sure she cares," Beka repeated.

"Why do you keep saying that?"

"Why do you keep talking to her like she can hear you?" Beka shot back.

Robbie gave a lovesick sigh. "I *wish* she could hear me – and answer." He glanced at Beka. "Don't you wish you could talk to her?"

"Not as much as you do."

"Do you think it's possible? I mean, do you think we could actually communicate with Jamie?"

"And scare her to death?"

"I guess you're right. It'd just be nice to talk to somebody besides *you*." Robbie gave her a playful smack on the shoulder.

"Talk to Jamie all you want. Just don't expect her to answer."

As they passed under Moosehead National Park's "welcome arch", Robbie told Jamie about the day – ten years ago – the arch was built, and how he and Beka had watched cranes lift metal beams into place.

The group wandered through the lodge area, around the shops and café, to the cabins in the foothills of Walrus Mountain, then on to the lake.

Beka gave up trying to talk to her tour-guide brother. She felt like a gooseberry. Like Robbie wanted to be "alone" with Jamie.

Finally she headed home. Thatch stayed with Robbie this time, which was fine. The dog needed to run and explore the forest bordering the lake more than he needed to go back to the house with her.

Along the way, Beka thought about the day they'd found Thatch in that same forest. She and Robbie had taken a path they'd never explored before when they heard faint sounds of crying. At first, they'd thought it was a baby.

The tiny cries had led them to the base of a tall larch pine. In a bed of crinkly leaves they had found a forlorn puppy, his tangled fur raggedy with twigs and burrs.

Robbie'd lifted the puppy from the leaves. They'd taken him home and given him bits of dried beef and water, then combed the burrs from his fur.

Beka had jokingly called him *Thatch*, because the puppy's fur reminded her of thatched huts in storybooks. The name stuck.

The twins had made a dog bed out of an old box. The next day, they'd taken Thatch to Dr Vetta in Juniper. He'd given the puppy shots, and shown the twins how to bathe him.

Dr Vetta had said Thatch's reddish markings against his white fur were *noble*. A true sign of a special dog. Beka liked to think of their dog as noble.

After putting an ad in the *Lost Pet* section of the *Juniper Daily News*, the twins had worried for a solid week, jumping each time the doorbell rang.

But no one ever came to claim Thatch.

Beka ran through the short cut, feeling the same rush of relief and pleasure she'd felt all those years ago when the lost puppy finally became a Zuffel.

In the back yard, she stopped at the gazebo, now feeling lonely. She *liked* the Makandas, especially Jamie, so it wasn't that.

What she *didn't* like, was losing her brother's attention.

Lonely or not, her new library books beckoned her to the attic. But now, the only way to get inside was to *smoosh* – the price she'd have to pay for not waiting for Jamie.

Hurrying to the veranda, Beka stood in front of the kitchen window. The glass sported a tiny hole, accidentally made years ago by Robbie's air rifle.

Her thoughts drew her inside. The warmth and comfort of the attic. The excitement of her books. Closing her eyes, she concentrated.

Dizziness swept over her, as though she'd been spun twenty times on the Whip at the Juniper carnival.

Pinpricks raced across her skin, giving her goose bumps.

A roaring sound filled her head, like a million winds blowing through the trees bordering Deer Creek.

Beka opened her eyes and gazed at the ceiling light in the kitchen.

She was inside.

Sitting up, she held her head until the *smooshing* headache disappeared.

Back to normal, she sprang to her feet, eager to get upstairs and settle down in a window seat to read.

But first...

What about Gran? Maybe she should check to make sure the woman was all right. Besides, Beka was curious about how a blind person could paint at all. How could she keep from making a mess on the canvas?

Beka pictured bodies with unconnected arms and legs.

Blue skies *below* mountain tops instead of above.

Trees growing out of roads or lakes instead of solid ground.

She tiptoed into the conservatory. Why she tiptoed, she wasn't sure, but entering the room made her feel as if she were trespassing into someone else's life.

Standing behind Gran, Beka was awestruck.

The picture taking shape on the canvas was

not out of kilter at all. The sky and trees were in their proper places.

Gran was filling in the sky with flecks of white and gold, plus streaks of red, pink, and grey.

Beka always thought the sky was blue – full stop. She never realized it held so much colour. Maybe she'd better take another look at the real thing.

She stepped closer. The painting looked familiar.

A grey house with dormers nestled among budding trees. A muddy drive curved up to a wide veranda.

"It's our house!" Beka stammered.

She smiled at the painting, as though the house were a friend she hadn't seen in years. "But it looks different," she added. "That's the way the house *used* to look. Decades ago. When it was painted grey, and the dirt drive was always muddy."

Now the house was white with green trim, and the drive was covered with gravel to end the muddiness.

"Wow," Beka whispered. "Gran is painting our house the way she remembers seeing it years ago."

She could hardly wait to show Robbie.

If she could get him to tear his eyes away from Jamie long enough to look at Gran's painting.

Chapter 7
Artist Talk

In two days, Gran painted four canvases. Besides the "early" Zuffel house, she'd painted:

Walrus Mountain in the days before ski runs were built.

The west shore of Kickingbird Lake, minus the piers and footpaths.

The main street of Juniper, including the town square with its bronze statue of the moose.

Beka had spent both days in the conservatory, reading and charting Gran's progress.

Something in the picture of Juniper captured her attention. Below the moose, etched in the concrete on the top step, was the image of a skull and crossbones. Beka didn't remember it being there.

Then she looked closer at the painting of Walrus Mountain. On the bottom part of the picture – in the same spot on the canvas as the crossbones – was a glass of water.

Beka was confused. What did it mean? It was obviously out of place.

In the painting of Kickingbird Lake, a branch, sporting dark berries, floated in the water between the west shore and Mystery Island.

If the branch was really there, it would be too small to see, but *this* branch was much bigger than its actual size. *It* confused Beka, too.

The back door slammed.

Robbie and Jamie were back from today's boat tour of Mystery Island.

Beka jumped into her book again, acting as though she hadn't been waiting for them. Thatch zoomed in, sliding on the slick wooden floor as he aimed for Beka, springing up to nuzzle her for a hug.

"Knock, knock," Jamie called before entering.

"Welcome back," Gran said. "Did you have fun?"

"Yes," Jamie answered. "I even remembered to buy canary food." Pulling a bag from her pocket, she filled the food trays in the bird-cage, chittering at Picasso and Dalí.

"Let me see what you've done," Jamie said, taking in the canvases. "Cool. Four finished paintings already!"

"Yes." Gran seemed pleased. "Mountain air gives me a wonderful surge of energy. Tell me if my pictures look as good as I think they do."

Jamie contemplated the view of the lake. "The detail of the forest is very sharp," she said. "I can't believe you painted this without—"

She winced at her unspoken words.

Beka suspected Jamie was careful about mentioning her grandmother's blindness.

"It's better than a Delacroix forest," Jamie finished.

Gran laughed. "I was aiming for a Monet."

"Huh?" Robbie gave her a puzzled look.

"Artist talk," Beka explained.

"What is the branch in the lake? Is it a symbol?"

"That's exactly what Bartholomew would ask."

Jamie shrugged. "Well, Mystery Island looks creepy and mysterious – just like a Van Gogh."

Gran nodded her approval.

Jamie leaned close to the next painting. "Is this a … a glass of water in the mountain scene?" She twirled to look at her grandmother, confused.

"I paint what I see in my mind's eye. It was there, so I sketched it."

Moving to the painting of the Zuffel house, Jamie quietly inspected it, as if looking for something else out of place. "The picture of the house needs children in it," she suggested. "Children with sweet faces."

"Sweet faces?" Beka made her daftest "sweet face" for her brother.

"And which artist draws sweet faces?" Gran asked.

Jamie squinted at the ceiling, thinking. "Botticelli?"

"Mmm, very good. I was thinking more of Cassatt, but Botticelli is a fine answer." Gran raised a paint-splattered thumb. "I've trained you well."

Jamie stopped in front of the painting of Juniper. "Hey, you put the moose in the town square."

"The square was *built* for that moose. Morty. That's what the townsfolk named him."

"But I stood on those very steps. The moose isn't there."

"I know." Gran leaned back in her chair. "I'm seeing Kickingbird the way it *used* to be. In the days before the moose disappeared."

"What happened to it?"

"Oh, my, I can't remember. It's been too long."

"Why didn't the police get the moose back?"

Gran put one hand to her head, as if it might help her remember. "I really can't say."

"Sis, look." Robbie pointed to the crossbones on the steps just as Jamie noticed them.

"What is this, Grandma Nell? A skull and crossbones? Scratched in the cement?"

"I told you, child. I paint what I see in my mind. And that's what I saw."

Jamie wrinkled her brow at the painting. "Well, *I* want to know what happened to the moose."

"So would we," Robbie told her. "So would everybody in Juniper."

"Do you mind if I go into town?" Jamie asked.

A smile spread across Gran's face. "You remind me of your father. Throw a mystery at him and he wouldn't stand still until it was solved."

Picking up a brush, Gran twirled it in turpentine, then wiped it on a rag. "Go ahead. See what you can find. The police have been on the moose case for as long as I can remember. Maybe they need someone like you to give it a fresh shot."

Jamie grinned, giving Gran a quick kiss. "Do you think I can solve the mystery of the missing moose?"

"Not without help," Robbie singsonged, motioning for Beka to come along with them.

"Not without *ghostly* help," Beka corrected, pleased to be asked to join Robbie and Jamie this time.

Thatch yipped to let them know *he* planned to help as well.

Chapter 8
The Moose-napper

First stop in Juniper was the mayor's office.

Beka had passed city hall many times, but she'd never ventured inside. The marble tile and granite columns were impressive. The cool air smelled of important documents and decisions.

The twins followed Jamie upstairs. Robbie kept a tight grip on Thatch.

At a reception area, Jamie asked a lady with a beehive hairdo if she could talk to the mayor.

The lady peered at the mayor's schedule. "Doesn't look good," she said. "He's a very busy man. Why don't you take a seat and I'll see what I can do. What's your name?"

Jamie glanced both ways before answering in a whisper.

At the name "Makanda", the beehive lady's eyebrows shot up three inches. Jumping from her desk chair, she scooped Jamie towards double oak doors and tapped lightly.

Opening the door, the lady shoved Jamie inside, not needing to offer any explanation.

The ghosts slipped through the opening with Jamie.

Mr Tavolott shot out of his chair when he saw her. "Is something wrong?" He grabbed his cowboy hat. "Do I need to go to the house?"

"Nothing's wrong," Jamie said. "I just need to ask you a few questions." She dropped her voice, suddenly acting shy in front of the lady.

Mr Tavolott waved his hand, and the woman left – with reluctance.

"What is it, Jamie?" He offered her a chair, then perched on the edge of his desk, still holding his hat.

"It's the moose, sir."

"The moose?"

"I, um, want to find out what happened to the moose that used to be in the town square."

Mr Tavolott rubbed his whiskers, as if this was the *last* question on earth he expected Jamie to come rushing into his office to ask.

"The moose." He stopped to remember. "The moose fell victim to a Hallowe'en prank. I can't remember when, but it's been at least forty years."

"Fifty," Beka said. "It happened before we became ghosts."

"A prankster was out that night, and thought it might be great fun to kidnap the Juniper moose, symbol of our great Moose-head Forest. This was before the forest became Moosehead National Park," he added.

"Whether or not the prankster meant for the moose to be returned, it never happened. Nor was the moose-napper – as he came to be known – ever found. The case was closed after all attempts to recover the statue failed.

And neither hide nor hair of the moose has ever been found." The mayor chuckled at his own cleverness.

"Gosh," mumbled Jamie.

"If you want to know more, go see Stan at the library. He can show you newspaper accounts. You can read the story."

"One more thing." Jamie paused, acting unsure how to word her next question. "What do the crossbones mean? The ones carved on the step?"

"I didn't know *anything* was carved on the step. Probably another prank." Mr Tavolott narrowed his eyes. "Why all this sudden interest in Juniper's missing moose?"

"One of Gran's paintings," she explained. "The moose was in the picture. I just wanted to know what happened to it."

Mr Tavolott came to his feet. "You mean, your grandmother is painting scenes of old Juniper?"

Jamie nodded. "And others, too. Kicking-bird Lake, Walrus Mountain, the Zuffel house."

"This is wonderful!" he gushed. "I must come and see them. Do you think your grandmother would mind?"

"I can ask her."

Mr Tavolott snatched a card off his desk and handed it to her. "Please call if it's OK. I'd love to see her work. Especially if she's drawing scenes from our own back yard. I've been a big Nell Makanda fan for years; even have one of her originals in my own house."

Jamie promised to let him know.

"Time to go," Robbie said. He was having a hard time keeping Thatch away from the sweets' dish on Mr Tavolott's desk.

Outside, Jamie headed straight for the town square. After waiting for the traffic light, she made her way to the concrete steps, now rising to nowhere.

The trio searched, step-by-step. The cross-bones were *not* there.

Jamie sat on top of the platform to rest. "Hmm," she said, which is exactly what Beka was saying to herself.

The twins sat on either side of her. Thatch

was busy exploring the steps – and dodging the traffic.

Suddenly a lightbulb clicked on in Beka's brain, throwing brightness into all the dark corners.

Clues!

The three symbols in the paintings were clues.

She'd read enough mystery books to know clues could be planted anywhere.

"Rob!" she hissed, leaning across Jamie. Or rather, *through* Jamie. "The crossbones, the water, and the branch!"

"What about them?" he asked before she could finish.

"They're clues! Clues to the whereabouts of the missing moose."

Some of her light spilled over into Robbie's brain. But before he could answer, Jamie shot to her feet.

"Clues!" the girl blurted, as though Beka's brainstorm had become her own. "They aren't symbols – they're clues!"

"Brilliant," Robbie exclaimed, gazing up at

Jamie with adoration.

"Hey, don't give *her* credit," Beka snapped, jabbing a thumb towards herself. "*I* figured it out first."

That's all she had time to say before scrambling to her feet and dashing after Jamie, who took off for home faster than Thatch could chase a squirrel up a tree.

Chapter 9
Ghostly Clues

Jamie and the twins sat on the veranda, watching nature paint the sunset as colourfully as Gran did. Thatch was busy chasing spring moths, which fluttered centimetres above the greening grass.

Jamie held a notepad and pencil. On the pad she'd written:

1. WATER
2. BRANCH
3. CROSSBONES

Chewing on her pencil, she stared at the words until Beka thought a hole might burn through the notepad.

"Water," Jamie began. "The *closest* water is the creek." She jabbed the pencil in the direction of Deer Creek, which angled through the Zuffels' back yard. "*Or* it could mean Kickingbird Lake – which is better known. I'll bet the moose is hidden somewhere near the lake."

"I agree," said Beka.

Next to WATER, Jamie wrote KICKINGBIRD LAKE.

"But the lake is huge," Robbie said. "We need to narrow it down."

"A branch," Jamie continued. "I'll bet it's a certain *type* of branch."

"It is," Beka told her. "Remember the berries?"

"The berries." Jamie tapped the pencil against her cheek. "How do I find out what kind of berries they are?"

"Ask Gran," Robbie suggested. "After all, she drew them."

Next to BRANCH, Jamie pencilled ASK GRAN.

Robbie's face lit up. "Hey, she listened to me."

"The answer was obvious." Beka yawned, acting bored with her brother's enthusiasm.

"And the crossbones. What do *they* mean? Death?" Jamie hugged herself, as if the word alone made her shiver.

"What about danger?" Robbie offered. "Crossbones could mean danger."

"Danger," Jamie echoed. "Maybe the moose is hidden in a dangerous place near the lake."

"Very good." Beka wished *she'd* been first to make the connections.

Robbie stood, leaning against the railing. "*Dozens* of spots around the lake could be considered dangerous."

"Maybe Gran would know the answer to that, too," Beka suggested.

Thatch raced across the veranda. Robbie roughed him up a bit before the dog dashed off to chase more moths. "Do you think Gran *knows* where the moose is hidden? I mean, why is she putting clues in her pictures? And how do we *know* they're clues?"

"I need to talk to Gran," Jamie blurted. Grasping her things, she rushed inside. The twins barely made it through the door.

Thatch didn't make it at all.

The instant he spotted the twins were inside, he sprang for the veranda, barking.

"Great," Robbie muttered. "Now, how do we get Thatch in?"

"He'll be all right," Beka said, not wanting to waste time. "Maybe we'll go out again, looking for more clues."

"Probably not. It'll be dark soon."

They hurried into Gran's studio. She was rough-sketching a scene with charcoal before adding paint.

"Hey," Jamie began, skipping her usual *Hello, how are you?* "What kind of branch is this?"

Gran stopped working and tilted her head. "It would help if you told me what you're looking at."

"Oh, sorry. It's the painting of the lake. There's a branch in the water. And it has berries on it. Where did it come from?"

"A bush."

Jamie rolled her eyes. "I'm serious."

Gran moved towards the painting, running her hands around the edge of the canvas, remembering through her fingertips what the painting looked like. "I don't know."

Jamie watched her grandmother, unsure of whether or not she was teasing. "How could you paint something and not know what it is or why you put it there?"

"Glory be, child, stop asking questions." She wiped her hands on her paint-splattered smock. "The branch was in the water, so I painted it. It's as simple as that."

"But it's out of perspective. It's far too big."

Gran held up one hand. "That's the way I saw it. End of argument."

Beka shivered. Something about Gran's feisty words stirred her. A sense of foreboding seemed to drop its veil over the darkening conservatory.

Robbie strode into the hallway. Had he felt it, too?

She followed him. He was in the kitchen, trying to get Thatch to *smoosh* inside for the night.

"Here, Thatch!" he shouted through the window.

The dog loped back and forth on the veranda, whining.

"Inside!" Beka called to him. "Come here."

The dog *wanted* to come into the house. He couldn't stand being separated from his master and mistress. Thatch's ghostliness made his dog loyalty even stronger. Seeing Robbie and Beka through the window was all the motivation he needed to *smoosh*.

A cold gust of wind hit Beka. She gasped for breath, realizing what it meant. When the whirlwind died, Thatch sprawled on the kitchen floor.

The twins fussed over him until he scrambled to his feet and gave them sloppy kisses.

Robbie knelt on the floor, quietly petting Thatch to calm him.

"Raz?" Beka began. "Did Gran's words make you feel…" Her voice trailed off. She couldn't find a word that described the feeling.

"Spooky?"

"That's a good word."

"I don't think Gran *knows* where those clues came from." He gave Beka a solemn look. "But I can't help thinking *somebody* put them into her mind."

Beka'd had the same hunch, but was afraid to mention it.

"I mean," her brother continued, "you and I know ghosts exist, right?"

She nodded, unsure whether or not she wanted to hear the rest of his conclusion.

"So, *I* think Gran sees the clues because somebody – who has powers like we do – showed them to her."

"I was afraid you were going to say that." Beka hugged herself to keep from shaking. "You really think a ghost has something to do with this?"

"Yes!" Robbie whispered. "And not just *any*

ghost. A ghost who knows where the missing moose is hidden."

Chapter 10
Hot on the Trail

In the morning, the twins found another clue.

Gran had stayed up late last night, painting a scene depicting the Juniper cemetery, which lay north-east of town.

It was the *old* Juniper cemetery, Beka noted. Giant oaks now shaded the graves, yet in the painting, they were saplings. And the picture's green, rolling hills were now covered with grave markers.

Everything in the scene was smudged, as if the viewer wasn't supposed to read the actual names and dates on the tombstones.

Except one.

That's why the twins decided it was a clue. Plus, the one word they *could* read didn't make any sense, as far as grave markers were concerned.

The letters looked like this:

N Ⓔ W Ⓢ

What did they mean? And why were two of the letters circled?

This morning, Robbie and Beka "haunted" the conservatory long before either of the Makandas were out of bed, trying to make sense of the picture.

"Maybe today's newspaper will tell us something," Robbie offered. "Maybe that's what NEWS means."

"Doesn't explain why the *E* and *S* are circled," Beka argued.

Sounds in the kitchen finally drew them away from the conservatory.

Jamie, already dressed and wearing a light jacket, hastily set breakfast items on a tray to carry into Gran's studio.

When she realized Gran wasn't up yet, she stopped rushing. Instead, she piled the Kickingbird brochures on the kitchen table, fanning them out to examine each one.

"OK," Jamie began. "Dangerous places near the lake. I've narrowed it down to three." She placed the brochures in order. "First, Mystery Island... Second, the path north of the lake, blocked by the sign that reads: 'CLOSED TO HIKERS'... Third, Danger Cove."

Robbie watched over Jamie's shoulder. "Good guesses. But she hasn't seen the new clue yet. How can we make sure she finds it?"

"She will," Beka assured him. "She always gives Gran her opinion of each painting."

Beka leaned her elbows on to the table to study the brochures. "I think Jamie picked three good places to start searching. If only we could narrow it down to one." She closed her eyes to think. "Too bad the new clue doesn't offer us directions."

Beka's words hit the twins at the same time.

"Directions!" they chimed.

Racing back to the conservatory, they gaped at the inscription.

"NEWS," Beka whispered. "It *could* stand for north, east, west, south."

"And east and south are circled," Robbie added. "Do you think it's a sign to look in the south-east corner of the lake?"

Beka mumbled Jamie's choices. "Mystery Island, the north path, Danger Cove."

"Danger Cove," Robbie repeated. "It's on the south-east end of the lake." He grinned, pleased with their sleuthing.

"*Woof!*" Thatch agreed, acting as if he'd known all along, if only they'd asked. Paws going a mile a minute, he raced from the room.

The twins followed him to the kitchen. He hunched by the door, waiting.

"Thatch is ready to go moose hunting," Beka said.

"So am I," Robbie added, too eager to stand still.

Jamie was pouring coffee into a thermos so Gran could have a hot cup whenever she wanted. Robbie stepped close, inhaling the aroma of brewed coffee with a blissful sigh.

Beka ignored him. He looked for any excuse to stand close to Jamie.

Carrying the thermos down the hall, Jamie tapped on Gran's door. "Morning," she called, peeking in.

Waiting for Gran to get up and come to breakfast was an exercise in patience. She'd slept in this morning since she'd worked long into the night.

While Gran ate, Jamie paced, glancing at the paintings, but not giving them enough attention to spot the message on the grave marker.

"She's ready to go moose hunting, too," Robbie said. "But if she doesn't notice the new clue, she'll waste a whole lot of time looking in all the wrong places."

Beka agreed. She wasn't sure how long the Makandas planned to stay in Kickingbird, but now that Jamie was hot on the trail of the moose, Beka hoped it could be found before the girl left.

She snapped her fingers. "I've got an idea."

Beka hustled Robbie to the kitchen. Thatch still waited by the door. "Soon, puppy," she cooed, placing her hands on Jamie's stack of brochures.

Waiting, Beka concentrated until she was able to pick all of them up – leaving only one behind. The one about Danger Cove.

A half hour later, Gran finished eating and dressing, then dismissed her granddaughter until lunchtime.

Jamie flew into the kitchen, stopping for the brochures. "Hey, where'd they go?" Frustrated, she snatched up the lone brochure. "'Danger Cove,'" she read. "Well, I guess that's a good place to start."

Shoving it into a small pack circling her waist, Jamie opened the kitchen door.

Thatch zoomed out so fast, he was almost a white blur.

"Thatch is acting strangely." Beka hurried to keep up with the dog – and Jamie – as they barrelled through the short cut. "Almost as if he knows what we're after. Do you think he does?"

"Need you ask?" Robbie teased. "Haven't you figured it out by now? With a ghost dog *anything* is possible."

Chapter 11
Going on a Moose Hunt

Spring played a trick on them.

The airy chirp of birds contradicted the chilly nip in the air, causing Jamie to rush back inside for a sweater.

Morning clouds darkened the sky, reminding the sun they still had a few more things to say before warm weather ruled.

Changes in the weather didn't bother the ghost twins. They simply waited for Jamie, then moved up the road to the lake in silence.

Even eager Thatch was quiet this morning, almost as if he, too, were pondering the meaning of the clues.

Jamie's sweater was the colour of cinnamon.

It matched her hair so well, Beka could hardly tell where it ended and the sweater began.

Beka wished her own hair was long and flowing like Jamie's, but it would never grow any longer than it was now. And it would never be red.

Robbie fell away from Jamie's side to walk with his sister. "If our hunch is correct," he began, picking up last night's conversation, "why would the ghost wait until now to point out the moose's hiding place?"

Beka had already figured it out. "Maybe he died before the moose was found, and he—"

"*He* could be a *she*," Robbie said, cutting in.

Beka poked him in the side for interrupting. "Maybe *the person* meant for the Hallowe'en prank to be a harmless joke. Maybe they intended for the moose to be found right away."

"And it wasn't."

"Right."

"So their conscience is bugging them from beyond the grave." Just saying the words sent chills across Beka's shoulders.

Robbie was quiet for a moment. "Good guess. But we'll probably never know where those clues came from."

Beka suddenly felt excited about their quest. "Wouldn't it be nifty if *we* found the moose?"

"We – and Jamie, you mean."

Beka rolled her eyes. "And Thatch, too. He hates being left out." She rested a hand on Thatch's head as they hiked.

The group passed Alpine Lodge, turning east to follow a footpath to the lake. Danger Cove lay several kilometres down a winding path that passed the boat launch and marina. The path also skirted the north edge of Rustic Hills Estates, the new suburb going up south of the lake.

Not many hikers ventured past Rustic Hills. From there on, the path angled sharply up-hill. Roots and rocks buckled out of the ground after years of rainstorms had carved the soft dirt away. Tripping and slipping were unavoidable.

Jamie slowed, stopping to catch her breath,

mumbling questions about why the path wasn't kept in better shape.

"Explain it to her, Raz," Beka said. "You've explained everything else."

Robbie took the opportunity to jog ahead to Jamie's side. "Most people come to the cove on a tour boat, wander around the pier, take pictures, climb the rocks, then get back on the boat."

He hopped over a fallen tree trunk. "We're taking the back route. Not many tourists come this way. I guess park rangers don't think the path needs fixing."

"Very good," Beka said. "Aren't you going to tell her why it's called Danger Cove?"

"She hasn't asked."

"*I'm* asking."

"Read the brochure," Robbie said. "The cove got its name after several boats smashed against rocks while trying to make it to shore. Now the safest route to the pier is marked by buoys.

"Also, a hiker slipped off a cliff, some campers disappeared, and countless horses have stumbled on the path, throwing their riders."

"Gee, I'm sorry I asked."

"Oh, I forgot about the bears."

"Bears?"

"There are more bear sightings here than anywhere else around the lake. I think it's because of the huckleberries that grow on the ledge. Anyway, bears tend to discourage hikers."

Beka waved her arm at him. "Spare me any more reasons why the place we're heading to is dangerous."

The group hit the top of a rise, catching their first sight of the cove.

On a sunny day, the sight would have been breathtaking. A forest cupped the half-circle of the cove, bringing trees almost to the waterline.

A small mountain of rocks cut the bordering trees in half. The trail ended on top of the boulders, so the group stair-stepped down to the pier.

The pier was in good shape. Tourist

information was available, plus a map for those who came to camp.

"Brave people," Beka whispered. She would *never* camp in bear territory.

Jamie sat on the pier, dangling her legs over the water.

Thatch went to work, investigating the area.

The twins waited to see what Jamie would do next.

"Water." Jamie jabbed a finger towards the lake. "We've got water. Next, a branch with berries." She glanced around. "There are zillions of bushes. I guess I need to find one with berries."

She squinted across the lake. "Crossbones," she said. "Danger. It *may* mean Danger Cove. Or there might be danger nearby – but I don't want to find out."

Rising, Jamie squinted at the sky. Behind clouds, the muted circle of sun was almost overhead. "I'm never going to make it back in time to fix Gran's lunch." She sighed. "Well, since I'm here, I'll take a quick look around, then start back."

Beka and Robbie had already begun poking about.

"Shout if you find a moose," Beka teased, climbing across the rocks to a dense grove of bushes.

"Too bad we can't show Thatch a picture of the moose, and tell him to go fetch," Robbie called back. "He'd find Morty in no time."

For the next half-hour, the group wandered the area west of the rocks, making wider and wider circles.

Beka kept one eye on Jamie, afraid the girl might start back without them, then stumble and fall on the rocky path – not that they'd be much help.

Giving up, Jamie folded her notes away, taking one last glance at the lake from the highest rock. "Not one branch here has berries," she grumbled. "I must be in the wrong place."

Beka was tempted to agree.

The group started back. This time, they cut south, passing Rustic Hills on the road to the Juniper Cemetery.

Beka hurried past the tall wrought iron fence surrounding the graveyard. This was *not* one of her favourite places.

As they passed the entrance gate, the last clue in Gran's painting popped into her mind: the headstone with the letters NEWS.

That headstone might be right inside this very gate. Maybe if she found it, she'd also discover the identity of the moose-napper.

The moose-napper who might now be a ghost.

Pausing by the gate, Beka tried to conjure up a little bravery. But all she felt was scared.

"Why are you stopping?" Robbie called.

"I'm going inside to see if I can find that grave. The one with the last clue." *Please come with me*, her mind begged.

Robbie stopped, as if trying to decide whether to help his sister or tag along with the girl of his dreams.

The decision was easy. "Good luck," he shouted with a quick wave. "Catch up with us later."

Beka's bravery fizzled out. Adventures were

easier with her brother along. Traipsing through the cemetery alone didn't seem like a whole lot of fun on such a gloomy day.

She clicked her tongue at Thatch. He broke away from the others and followed her through the gate.

"Thank you, puppy," she said, relieved.

Pushing unpleasant thoughts away, Beka felt overwhelmed at the number of graves fanning out before her. She gave a deep sigh, which sounded loud in the eerie stillness.

Starting off, she hurried along the drive, trying to ignore the quivers racing up and down her spine.

And – trying to ignore the eerie hunching of Thatch's back as his fur slowly rose on end.

Chapter 12
A Grave Mistake

The path Beka followed wove through graves like streets in Rustic Hills wove through houses. But here, the homes were permanent. Ha!

She groaned at her own creepy joke.

Inside the cemetery, the air was quiet, as if the birds whose songs filled the air along the road from the lake hushed the moment their flight took them over the graveyard fence.

Beka gazed into tall trees lining the drive. Yes, birds perched on the branches. But they were silent. *That's odd*, she thought.

Or was it just her imagination?

Thatch was practically glued to her side.

Beka hoped he was staying close because he felt protective – not because he was scared, too.

A frightened ghost dog was a worthless watchdog.

Closing her eyes, Beka pictured the cemetery in Gran's painting. If she could remember the exact scene, maybe she could locate the grave marker quickly.

That way, she wouldn't have to look at every single grave – an impossible task since hundreds of headstones dotted the rolling hills.

The deeper Beka ventured into the cemetery, the more tingles shivered up and down her spine.

Yet, if anybody was here, shouldn't *they* be afraid of *her*?

After all *she* was a *ghost*.

Lots of ghosts might be hanging around here. It's a cemetery.

"Thanks," she mumbled to her imagination. Sometimes she wished it wasn't so vivid.

Beka slowed. She really wasn't in the mood to run into another ghost. Maybe she'd better do what she came to do, then scarper.

Taking a sharp right turn, she moved among headstones, peering at each one, searching for the mysterious clue.

Names and dates stood quietly at attention on each marker.

Some quoted poems or Bible verses, or even displayed pictures of the grave's occupant. But none held a secret message carved in one corner.

Beka thought about the concrete steps in the town square, leading up to the moose statue that was no longer there. When she and the others had searched the steps, the cross-bones were nowhere to be found.

So maybe there *wasn't* a secret clue carved into any of the stones. Maybe the clues existed only in Gran's paintings.

"I'm wasting my time," she grumbled. "I'm scaring myself for no good reason."

A soft, rattling noise stopped her.

Beka twirled, half expecting to see a ghost behind her.

Only the ghost in her imagination didn't

look like a normal person. Didn't look like her – or Robbie.

The image lunging into her mind was a collection of ghosts and monsters from all the scary books she'd read and all the scary movies she'd watched. *Yikes!*

Beka squinted down the path. What she *actually* saw was Thatch, teeth bared, nose wrinkled. Growls echoed in rhythm from his throat. Every muscle tensed, as if he was about to pounce on … what?

Beka followed his gaze. The dog's eyes were definitely locked on something. All *she* saw were rolling hills, trees, and graves.

Thatch's ghost powers had always been stronger than hers and Robbie's. (That was one of the *Ghost Rules* she'd made up long ago when the twins were learning what they could and couldn't do.)

Beka didn't doubt for one moment that Thatch could actually *see* whatever danger lay ahead. A danger she could only *feel*. And that feeling had been with her ever since she'd stepped through the iron gate.

Whatever Thatch was protecting her from loomed directly ahead.

"It's OK, puppy," she whispered, retreating. "We'll leave now."

Thatch backed up with her. Good. The *thing* would know they were leaving. That should appease whoever – or whatever – blocked their way.

When Beka reached the paved drive, an overwhelming urge made her break into a run. It reminded her of the "hurry up" feeling that nagged her whenever she took the short cut home by herself.

The path through the sand plums was always shadowed. When Robbie was with her, it wasn't a problem. But alone, she could never walk through. Something always pushed her into a run the moment she stepped into the shadows.

Something was pushing her now.

Thatch gave a growl-bark, sounding like he meant business. Like he was telling *whatever* not to follow, or IT would have an angry ghost dog to deal with.

Beka bolted. All she could think about was getting out of there. Getting to safety.

Thatch galloped behind, racing so close he almost tripped her.

Rounding the last corner, Beka flew towards the gate.

It was closed.

She gasped. The gate had been open when she entered the cemetery.

Who had closed it? How was she supposed to get out? The fence was three metres high.

She slowed, but Thatch kept moving. In one smooth leap, he sailed over the fence.

"Wow!" Beka watched in awe, amazed at the sight of Thatch's superdog powers.

Then it hit her. Thatch was *outside* – but she was still *inside*. Trapped.

Now what?

On the other side of the fence, Thatch paced, acting confused. Had he expected Beka to leap the fence with him?

Grasping the iron bars, horror sent dizziness flooding through her until she felt faint.

Was IT pounding the drive after her this very moment?

Terrified, Beka screamed, "Puppy, don't leave me here!"

Chapter 13
The Ghost's Warning

S moosh! Beka's mind screamed at her.

"I can't!" she screamed back.

Smooshing demanded total concentration. How could she focus with IT breathing down her neck?

Beka wouldn't allow her mind to imagine what IT might be.

Possible solutions tumbled through her brain as she tried to climb the fence. But the iron posts were slippery and too thin to grasp. Toeholds in the swirly designs decorating each post were too narrow for her shoes.

If Thatch can jump the fence, you can, too.

At first Beka tried to ignore the impossible

idea. Yet, didn't the idea agree with one of her ghost rules? *Sometimes Thatch teaches us things we didn't know we could do.*

Beka chanced four giant steps backward. Ignoring the panic choking her, she quick-counted to three, then took a running step and jumped with all her might.

She didn't quite clear the fence. Still, she was able to throw one leg over the top and grasp the railing between two sharp spikes capping each post.

Having Thatch cheer her on would have been helpful. Yet he wasn't even watching her. He was staring at the path where she'd stood moments before. Staring at whatever had thrown him into his attack mode.

Teetering on the top railing as though it were a monkey bar, she dared a glance. Dared to look at whatever held Thatch's attention.

What she saw appeared and disappeared so quickly, at first Beka thought she imagined it.

A shimmer. A cloud. A mist. There on the path.

A wispy frame, moving with every *whoosh*

of the breeze, as if nothing but a "mission" could keep it from blowing away with the dandelion puffs.

And Beka had given the *thing* its mission.

To issue a warning.

From one ghost to another.

An arm extended. A bony finger pointed at Beka.

The message was brief, and not even spoken. The words simply exploded inside her mind, yet she knew the *thing* put them there: *Find what's missing; never mind the thief.*

Beka swung her leg over the railing and let go, dropping three metres on to the road outside the fence as smoothly as if she'd dropped one metre.

Thatch immediately tugged at her shirt, urging her to make a fast getaway to safety.

But her eyes stayed fixed on the swirling mist as it melted into thin air.

Find what's missing; never mind the thief.

So. She and Robbie had been right. Who-ever was responsible for the missing moose was being haunted by his own conscience. He wanted the moose found. But he didn't want his name to be known.

"Fine," Beka said out loud, agreeing to the ghost's terms.

Being brave was easier outside the gate with Thatch at her side. Being brave was easier when she didn't have to face the swirly mist.

"Why wasn't it afraid of me?" she asked out loud. Pondering the question, she knelt to hug Thatch. "Could the ghost see me like I am? Or was I nothing more than a mist to him?"

Thatch's intense eyes seemed to be pondering her questions, too.

"Could I have scared him if I wanted to?" If Robbie were here, she might have tried, but facing another ghost alone was too unnerving.

A sudden urgency came over her. Rising to her feet, Beka dashed down the road towards Juniper and home.

Being a ghost was a complicated prospect. Someday she hoped to find answers to the ghost issues that baffled her.

* * *

Beka found Robbie waiting for her at the fork in the road where Juniper's main street split into Aspen and Deer Creek.

When Thatch spotted his master, he zoomed ahead, jumping up on Robbie with tiny *yips* and *yaps*, as if saying, "Guess what happened to us?"

Robbie gave him a good rubbing, then frowned at Beka. "What took you so long? I've been waiting for ever." He studied her face. "Hey, what's wrong?"

"Nothing." Beka felt pleased that her brother had left Jamie's side long enough to come out and greet her. But she wanted to be fussed over, too, like Thatch – not scolded.

She started towards the house, but Robbie stopped her.

"You can't hide stuff from me, Sis; I've known you too long. Something happened. You look terrible; like you've seen a ghost."

She set her hands on her hips. "I'm looking at one right now."

"Whoops," he said, grimacing. "Bad choice of words."

She laughed at the irony. "Actually, you hit the nail on the head."

Quickly, Beka filled him in on her adventure in the cemetery.

The look on Robbie's face fell somewhere between amazement at Beka's story and guilt over not being there. "I should have stayed with you. He might not have messed with *two* of us."

"Well, forget him," she said. "The point is, now we know what the clues mean. All we have to do is help Jamie figure them out."

"And fast," Robbie added.

Oh, no. Beka feared this was coming sooner or later. "Are they going home?"

He nodded. "Day after tomorrow."

"Whoa. It doesn't leave us much time to find the missing moose." Beka spoke the words loud and clear – just in case the graveyard ghost was listening. *And* in case he felt like making their search a little easier...

Chapter 14
Kickingbird, the Early Years

By early afternoon, the sun broke through the gloom, warming the land and the breeze. By the time the twins returned home, Jamie had propped the kitchen door open.

Beka loved being able to stroll in and out whenever she pleased. Closed doors were always such a bother.

Robbie hurried her to the conservatory, eager to show her something.

Gran, wearing a blue paint smock, perched on her chair at the easel, dabbing green paint on to a canvas.

Beka wondered if the smell of paint and turpentine would ever leave the room after the Makandas went home.

She followed Robbie to a finished painting that was leaning against the far window to dry.

He waited for her reaction.

Beka studied the picture. A forest scene. The lake shimmered in the far background. Trees and shrubs hunched on each side of the canvas, melting into a central meadow bursting with early spring flowers.

Rocks bordered one side of the meadow, but the complete scene was hard to take in because of the figures blocking the view.

The figures of a boy and girl.

"It's you and me!" Beka yelped. "Gran painted *us*!"

She stared at the picture of herself. How long had it been since her image looked solid, the way it was in the painting?

Beka reached out to touch her face on the canvas, then pulled her hand away. What if the paint was still wet? She wouldn't want to smudge it.

She peered at her clothes: a pink and navy checked sundress, falling just below the knees. In one hand, she held a navy jacket.

"I remember this outfit. I'd got it for summer, but wanted to wear it earlier. I took the jacket that day because it's always chillier by the lake."

Robbie wore dark trousers and a long sleeved green shirt. Beka didn't remember his clothes at all. One hand was raised above his head, pointing at something in the background. Whatever it was, their images blocked it from view.

"What's that on your shirt?"

"My Superman badge," Robbie answered. "I noticed it instantly."

Beka squinted at the scenery. "Where *are* we?"

"I haven't figured it out yet. Somewhere around the lake. We went so often, I can't remember this time in particular."

Beka agreed. It could have been one of a million trips to the lake.

"Have you noticed any clues? I mean, do you think you're pointing at something important?"

"Maybe. But until we figure out the location, it's not going to mean much."

"Who are *they*?"

Beka jumped. She'd been so intent on the painting, she hadn't heard Jamie step up behind them.

"Who, dear?"

"Oh, sorry. I'm looking at the painting by the far window. It's a view of the lake, with two kids in the foreground, and a dog in the background."

A dog? Beka's gaze danced around the picture. *Yes! There's Thatch.* She hadn't even noticed him.

Gran held a paintbrush in mid-air, thinking. "That was the oddest thing. I painted that scene of the lake from memory, when these children came breezing along and stopped in the middle of the picture."

Feeling for the rag-covered table next to her, she set down the brush and lifted a tea bag out of a cup. "It was almost as if the children stopped to pose for me – or to tell me to look at something behind them."

She took a sip of tea. "Nearly left out the dog, though; he wouldn't stand still long enough for me to get his colouring right."

Thatch's image *was* blurred, so what Gran said rang true.

Beka noticed Thatch's back. It was hunched in the stance he took whenever he sensed a threat. In this case, the threat was whatever Robbie was pointing at.

"He's cute," Jamie exclaimed.

At first Beka thought Jamie was talking about Thatch. Then the girl traced Robbie's outline in the air with one finger, as if noting how Gran had drawn him into the picture.

Robbie's face grew bright red. He turned away so Beka couldn't see.

"I wonder what the boy's name is?" Jamie asked. "Do you think he lives around here?"

Gran set down her teacup. "Aren't you a bit young to be boy crazy?"

"Grandma Nell!" Jamie acted shocked.

She chuckled. "Since all my other paintings are of *old* Kickingbird, I'd say the boy lived a long time ago. Can't you tell by his clothes?"

"Not really. They look normal to me. And the girl's outfit is cool."

"Thank you," Beka said, grinning.

"Cool?" Gran repeated. "*I* used to wear sundresses like hers, but I never thought my granddaughter would think they were *cool*."

The doorbell rang.

Gran froze, brush in hand, ready to start again. "Who could that be?"

"Oh," Jamie slapped two fingers to her lips. "I almost forgot. I told Mr Tavolott he could come by and look at your paintings."

Her grandmother didn't answer.

"Is it OK?" Guilt coloured Jamie's face. "He's your old friend, isn't he?"

"Well, he already knows I'm painting, so I guess he deserves a look," Gran said with a sigh. "It's fine, dear. Let the man in."

Jamie rushed to the entry hall. In a few seconds, she returned with Mr Tavolott, cowboy hat in hand.

He squeezed Gran's shoulder in greeting. "Dear Nell, I was so pleased to hear your work is going well. And to hear *what* you're painting. May I have a look?"

"Be my guest."

Touring the room, he stopped to *ooh* and *ahh* each painting, as Jamie pointed out all the highlights. "These are wonderful," he gushed.

Gran leaned back, crossing her arms to bask in the attention.

Mr Tavolott yanked a chair next to hers and straddled it backwards. "As mayor of Juniper, I want to declare Saturday *Nell Makanda Day*. We're dedicating our new community room at the Sugarberry Library. We can display your paintings, and call it *Kickingbird, the Early Years*. How about it?"

Jamie gave a little gasp. "Oh, Gran, that would be super."

"Charles Tavolott." Gran rose from her chair, refusing his offer of assistance. "Have you broken our agreement? My presence here is a secret."

"Course I haven't broken our agreement." He seemed offended. "But what you've done in this room the past week is too good not to share with the community." He marvelled again at the paintings. "Nell, you owe this to the place of your birth."

Gran felt for the easel to steady herself.

Mr Tavolott rushed to take her arm. "Besides, how long has it been since you've had a showing of your art? You love showings, remember? You love it when people adore you and your work."

"Humph. I'm having a showing next week, for your information. Bartholomew scheduled it long before my stroke."

"But *you're* not going to be there," Jamie reminded her. "Just your paintings."

"Why not?" she argued. "The sponsors have been begging me to make an appearance. Bartholomew says Miss Bronzino won't take *no* for an answer."

"You mean we're going?" Jamie blurted. "To the Uffizi?"

"Certainly." Gran cocked her head as if she'd made up her mind at that moment. "Returning to work in this glorious mountain air has made me feel ten years younger."

"Good thing it doesn't make *us* feel ten years younger," Beka whispered. "We'd be ghost babies!"

Robbie didn't laugh at her joke. "How far away is the Uffizi?" he said instead, looking panic-stricken at the thought of Jamie leaving.

"Um, what is the Uffizi?" Mr Tavolott asked, echoing Robbie's concern.

"It's an art museum," Gran told him. "In Florence?"

"Florence?" Robbie repeated. "Where's that?"

"You mean, we're flying to Italy?" Jamie jumped up and down three times.

Gran nodded. "We'll go home Saturday night to get ready, then fly out on Sunday."

"Italy?" Robbie slumped into a chair.

Beka patted his shoulder. "Don't worry, Raz. You've still got me."

"What about Dr Tekoa?" Jamie asked.

"I'll send her a lovely postcard from Europe."

Mr Tavolott gave a hearty laugh. "Well, then, *our* showing will be Saturday afternoon. You won't have to change your travel plans."

He plopped his hat on with authority. "If

you're venturing back into the public eye, a small showing here in Juniper will be good practice; will get you back in the swing of things."

"Oh, Charles." She let him guide her to the chair. "You're so good at getting your own way. I know from the days when I babysat for you."

Beka found *that* hard to imagine.

"It will take me all day tomorrow to finish enough paintings to call it a showing. They'll be dry and ready to go by noon on Saturday. Meanwhile, no more interruptions. And please, Charles," she added, "ask Bartholomew to arrange our trip and fax a message to Miss Bronzino to tell her we're coming."

"Yes, ma'am!" Mr Tavolott hurried from the room, firing back orders. "Get to work, now. Jamie, keep distractions away from her. I'll be over with a truck to move the paintings to the library." Then he was gone.

Robbie still slumped in the chair, gazing at Jamie, a forlorn look wrinkling his forehead.

"Cheer up," Beka said, nudging him. "Our picture is going to be on display at the library! We're going to be famous!"

Chapter 15
What a Ghost Dog Was Meant to Do

Noises from downstairs drew Beka from the attic long before sunrise.

Gran was already up, working in the dark – which didn't bother her, of course.

Settling on to the built-in bench, Beka scanned Jamie's art books, filling her mind with chapters on colour wheels and palette knives. How to keep sketchbooks and shade with charcoal. How to create shadows and clean paint from brushes.

Reading about drawing and painting made her wish she could try it.

" 'Morning." Jamie tiptoed into the conservatory with Gran's coffee thermos. She set it down gingerly, not wanting to break Gran's concentration.

"Mmm," was all her grandmother answered, so Jamie tiptoed out.

Beka worried her *own* presence might be distracting the artist. If Gran had sensed the ghost twins enough to "see" them in her mind, could she now sense Beka's nearness?

Imitating Jamie, Beka tiptoed from the conservatory.

For the rest of the morning, everyone left Gran alone.

Jamie retreated to her room to sketch, and the twins stayed in the attic, playing cards with a deck left behind by a former Zuffel house guest.

At least once every hour they slipped downstairs to check on Gran's progress – and to see if she'd added any more clues.

In the afternoon, the doorbell rang.

Startled, the twins hurried to the front windows.

"Look!" Beka pointed at the line of vans turning up the drive. Vans with wires and other strange contraptions sitting on top.

Thatch's ears flew up at the sight.

"Let's go," Robbie said.

Downstairs, Jamie was stationed at the front door. Half a dozen people crowded around her, holding cameras and thrusting microphones into her face.

"Please go away," Jamie was saying.

"Just tell us if it's true," a gum-chomping reporter asked, vying for a spot next to Jamie. "Tell us if Nell Makanda is really here."

Jamie looked as if she might cry.

"Leave her alone," Robbie growled in the reporter's face.

Thatch growled, too, so Robbie caught hold of him.

"We've got to do something," Beka said. "If the reporters distract Gran, she'll *never* finish the paintings, which means—"

"We'll *never* find the rest of the clues," Robbie finished.

"Right."

The breeze blew Robbie's hair over his eyes, so he shoved it back. "And if we don't find the final clue before tomorrow, Jamie will be gone." He sighed.

Beka wasn't sure if he was sighing over the clues or Jamie. "Our chances of finding the moose will be gone, too," she added, wondering if the graveyard ghost would be angry if they failed in their quest.

"You can't stay here," Jamie told the growing crowd. "You can't make any noise."

"Ah, so it's true," another reporter blurted. "The artist *is* here. And she needs peace and quiet."

The crowd mumbled their agreement.

The gum-chomper finally wormed his way next to Jamie. "And who are *you*?" he asked.

"I'm…" Jamie paused.

"Don't tell him," Beka shouted, inches from the girl's ear. "It's none of his business."

Jamie held her tongue and said no more.

"Good girl," Beka muttered, giving the reporter a shove. Too bad her hand went right through his arm.

"We can't let them get past Jamie," Robbie said. "Gran would really be upset." He glanced at Beka. "Do you think we can make them leave?"

"Leave?" She shrugged. "I don't know. But we *can* distract them." Beka had done enough "distracting" to know it worked. *How* it worked, she wasn't sure. And she'd never tried it before on a whole crowd.

Vans were parking all over the front yard, while TV crews set up equipment.

Some were already filming the front of the house, while on-camera reporters gave background information about Nell Makanda and her link to Kickingbird: How she'd disappeared after her stroke, and refused to talk to the media. And how a press release announcing a special showing of Makanda art accidentally leaked to other media sources.

"Let's split up," Beka suggested. "Do all you can to distract them."

Robbie let go of Thatch's collar. "Guess there's no need to hold him back any more."

At the same instant, a squirrel shimmied down a post of the veranda.

With a delighted *yip*, Thatch was off, giving

the startled squirrel the chase of his life.

Beka giggled, watching the squirrel zigzag between crews – Thatch hot on his trail. She knew the squirrel couldn't *see* the dog; it sensed him and ran. "This is what a ghost dog was meant to do."

"Thatch!" Robbie shouted, urging him on. "Do your stuff."

Reporters jumped from the path of the crazed squirrel. Equipment toppled. Screams and hollers filled the air as the confused animal backtracked through the crowd, searching for a way out.

Jamie used the distraction as an opportunity to slip into the house and close the door.

Good, Beka thought, hoping Gran couldn't hear all the commotion.

"What are we waiting for?" Robbie cried. "Let's help!"

Beka made a beeline towards the gum-chomper. He was untangling cables that the squirrel and Thatch had tangled. Beka stepped on his shoes. "Go home!" she shouted. "Leave these nice people alone. Go away. Go away."

She chanted the words over and over.

The reporter stopped fiddling with the equipment. Squinting at the sky, he mumbled, "Temperature must have dropped ten degrees in five seconds." Diving into the van, he dug out a jacket. The emblem read KBTV, which stood for the local Kickingbird station.

"The temperature didn't drop," Beka snarled. "You've been *iced* by a ghost."

Thatch finally chased the squirrel up a tree on the other side of the road. Trotting back, head high with pride, he stumbled on to a reporter's lunch, sitting on an equipment bag. Thatch wolfed it down.

Who was dumb enough to leave an unguarded hamburger in the presence of a ghost dog?

Across the yard, Robbie danced and sang in front of a camera. The girl filming the area kept stopping to check the view and clean the lens. Beka wondered what she saw. A wispy ghost puff clouding her view?

Reporters banged on the front door of the Zuffel house, but Jamie refused to open it again.

The twins and Thatch moved around the yard, bugging everyone in turn until the crews packed up and left.

When the last van pulled out, Beka shook hands with her brother. "Good job of haunting, Raz."

"*Woof!*" Thatch barked.

"You too, puppy."

"Only one problem." Robbie nodded towards the front window where Jamie peeked out, looking surprised to find the front yard empty. "Now *we're* locked out, and it's *our* house."

Beka laughed. "Thank heavens for opened back doors."

Chapter 16
Searching for the Final Clue

At noon on Saturday, as promised, Mr Tavolott barrelled up the drive in a truck large enough to move an entire house full of furniture.

Gran was packing away brushes, paint tubes, smocks, and rags in the steamer trunk. Jamie helped her fold easels and take drop cloths up off the floor.

Soon the conservatory looked the way it did when they arrived.

Jamie grabbed a broom, pausing to inspect each of the eight finished paintings as she swept.

"You're certainly interested in your grandmother's work," Mr Tavolott said, folding the extra table and chairs, moving them out of the way.

Jamie swept faster, acting like she'd been "caught" studying the paintings too closely.

"My granddaughter likes to compare me with the masters," Gran explained. "She sends me off to bed without supper if my colours aren't as bold as Matisse's, or if I don't use proper balance like Degas."

"Gra-an," Jamie said. "That's not true."

Beka knew the real reason Jamie was scrutinizing the paintings. She was searching for the final clue. The one that would clinch the whereabouts of the moose.

Which is exactly what Beka was doing.

Why had the clues stopped after her "run-in" with the moose-napping ghost in the cemetery?

Was it *her* fault the final clue had never come?

Beka toured the conservatory, troubled by her thoughts.

Had the ghost changed his mind about the

twins and Jamie finding the moose? Was he giving clues to other kids who lived in Juniper? Maybe they were out right now searching for the hidden treasure.

No, Beka's mind told her. Kids today didn't even *know* about the missing moose. Jamie had learned of it only by coincidence.

Or *was* it coincidence?

After helping Jamie fold drop cloths, Gran left to get "spruced up", as she called it.

Robbie wandered into the conservatory. A two-day-old frown lingered on his face. Beka hadn't seen him this sad since the time he thought he'd lost Thatch on a camping trip deep in the Moosehead Mountains.

Mr Tavolott helped Jamie wrap each canvas in cloth to protect it for the trip to town.

"Look," Beka said. "Thatch is saying good-bye to Picasso and Dalí."

Thatch balanced on his hind legs on the bench. One paw rested against the window; the other dangled in mid-air. He lifted his nose to sniff at the birds.

The canaries flapped their wings,

attempting to flee. Their chirps turned throaty, as if they were scolding something. Something like a ghost dog? Could birds sense Thatch's presence? Like squirrels and cats?

Gran's cane tapped on the floor as she returned. "Goodness, what's got into my canaries? Jamie, cover the cage so Charles can take it to the truck."

Jamie did, but the birds kept scolding until Thatch hopped down.

Gran was dressed in a ruffly spring dress the colour of newborn chicks. A matching yellow hat perched on top of her head.

"Fetch your things, dear, so we can make our public appearance." The tone of her voice turned sarcastic on the words *public appearance* – which wasn't lost on Mr Tavolott.

"You're an angel for doing this, Nell," he told her. "We have a big surprise for you this afternoon to make it all worth your while."

"I hate surprises," she grumbled.

The twins and Thatch hitched a ride in the

cab of the truck for the short trip into Juniper. It was a tight squeeze. Mr Tavolott turned on the heat to remove the "ghost chill".

Outside the library, a huge crowd waited to greet the artist.

"Doesn't look like one single person showed up to see you," Mr Tavolott teased.

"Humph."

Beka couldn't tell whether Gran was pleased or insulted.

Giggling, Jamie whispered the truth into Gran's ear.

"Humph," she said again, her lips curling into a satisfied smile.

Mr Tavolott parked the truck in the back alley so workers could unload the paintings and set them up for the show.

Also parked behind the library was a rented limo so Gran could arrive out front in style. But she'd have nothing to do with it.

"I'll go in the back door with my work," she insisted.

"Ohhh," Robbie moaned. "I think Thatch *really* wanted to ride in a limo. Right, boy?"

Thatch bobbed his head, almost as if he were agreeing.

Mr Tavolott helped Gran and Jamie out of the truck.

Gran paused in the alley, shoving her hat to one side. "Jamie, dear, tell your old grand-mother how gorgeous she looks."

Jamie straightened the hat back the way it was, fussing over Gran's clothes. "There," she finally said. "The famous artist is ready for her first showing in ... golly, in *months*."

Mr Tavolott offered his arm, placing Gran's through his. "Madam Makanda," he proclaimed, "your adoring public awaits you."

Gran didn't *humph* this time.

Chapter 17
The Showing

Beka stepped through the back door of the community room, remembering the last time she'd been there: Juniper's first cat show.

Thanks to Thatch, it might become Juniper's *last* cat show.

The front doors hadn't been opened yet, so the room was empty of people. On one side, the eight paintings, still covered, were arranged on easels. On the other side was a small stage. Across the front sat a buffet table piled high with finger food and punch.

A huge banner proclaiming WELCOME was stretched across one wall.

The instant Beka noticed the food, she

grabbed Thatch and held on tight. She could *not* allow the ghost dog to ruin Gran's special moment.

Jamie wandered about the room, looking lost and forgotten – and depressed.

Beka knew Jamie was blaming herself for not finding the moose – or the final clue. Yet it wasn't her fault. *Beka* was the one who'd let her own curiosity mess up Jamie's plan. She wished she could apologize.

Mr Tavolott dashed about the room, giving last-minute orders, checking the microphone, even sampling the punch to make sure it was icy.

He stationed Gran on the stage in a chair, then called for the doors to be opened.

People flowed into the room as if a dam had broken. They gathered around the stage, leaving room in front for reporters and cameras. The gum-chomper was first to set up, Beka noticed.

Mr Tavolott greeted everyone, giving a short talk about the building of the community room, and what a great honour it was to be hosting a showing of Nell Makanda's art.

"And now," he continued, "before we unveil the paintings, I'd like to announce the judges' unanimous decision for the name of our new community room. From this day forth, the room shall be called the *Makanda Room*."

Cheers and applause filled the air. Gran placed a hand over her heart, truly pleased. She thanked Mr Tavolott, the judges, and the audience, then urged everyone to help themselves to dessert and a "peek at her paintings".

The crowd obeyed, collecting treats and moving across the room.

A librarian stepped quickly down the line of paintings, removing the cloths. More applause skittered through the room, with the appropriate *oohs* and *ahhs*.

"There we are," Beka yelped, tugging Robbie's arm. "Our painting is last in line."

The twins hurried over, with Beka half-dragging Thatch away from the buffet table. She couldn't wait for the crowd to reach the final painting. To hear their reactions to the "children" in the lake scene.

Robbie seemed excited, too, which meant he was getting over his lovesickness. At least that's what Beka *hoped* it meant.

As she gazed with pride at her own image on the canvas, an odd thing began to happen. Her image paled, then began to fade.

"Raz!" she hissed. "What's happening?"

They gaped at the picture until Beka was completely invisible.

Next the image of Thatch turned wispy and faded away. Thatch whined and cocked his head, as if he, too, was confused.

Finally, the image of Robbie lightened. Going … going … gone!

"Wow," he whispered, staring at the canvas as if he expected the figures to return. "Gran *saw* us when she was in our home. Our images were strong there." He glanced at Beka. "But *away* from the house—"

"We disappear," she finished in a solemn voice.

Both were silent, but neither could come up with a better explanation.

By the time the crowd reached the last painting, no children smiled at them from the canvas.

"Oh, my gosh!" came Jamie's voice.

Beka twirled. Had the girl seen it happen?

"They're gone," Jamie whispered. Her freckles looked dark against her suddenly pale face.

"Oh, great," Robbie muttered. "She has no idea what's going on. And we have no way of telling her."

Beka watched Jamie's stunned expression, feeling sorry for shocking her – not that it was the twins' fault.

Slowly Jamie raised a hand and pointed at the painting. "There it is," she gasped. "Finally."

"There *what* is?" Beka turned to study the canvas again.

Instantly, she saw what Jamie was gaping at. With the twins out of the way, the background came into full view.

What Robbie had been pointing at was now visible.

Almost hidden by rocks – and overgrown

huckleberry bushes – peeked the entrance to a small, dark cave.

"It's the final clue!" Beka and Jamie cried in unison.

Chapter 18
I Think We Have Company

After a few quick whispers to Gran, Jamie flew out the door. The twins had to hustle to keep up with her.

Thatch sensed Jamie's urgency, zooming on ahead with her.

They raced due north, through some of Juniper's quaint neighbourhoods, then past the cemetery.

Beka didn't dare glance through the fence, afraid to see what she'd seen before on the path. Somehow she felt the graveyard ghost knew what was happening right now, and had even hidden the final clue in such a clever way to keep them guessing till the end.

Beka didn't think it was funny.

They barrelled on past Rustic Hills, then down a sloping wooded hillside ending on the rocks at Danger Cove. Since they'd already searched west of the cove, the group turned east, their minds in agreement.

They hiked, scanning the countryside until the scene opening out before them matched the one in Gran's painting.

"This is it!" Jamie cried. "The meadow; the trees. And somewhere in those rocks is the entrance to the cave. Yes, a cave!" she added, doing a little hop-step on the path. "A cave would be the *perfect* place to hide something big and heavy. Like a moose."

"Brilliant!" Robbie exclaimed.

Beka *tsked* at him. "Hey, I figured it out, too, and you didn't call *me* brilliant."

"We know *you're* brilliant," he said. "You have to be. You're my twin."

"Ha!" Beka gave him a playful punch.

With a throaty growl, Thatch dashed off across the meadow, already dotted with red and yellow wild flowers.

"Does he know where we're going?" Beka whispered.

"Never underestimate the power of a ghost dog," Robbie said, returning her punch.

Before she could respond, Robbie took off, following Thatch's path through the moist grass.

Jamie was already making her way across the meadow, beating them to the rocks.

As Beka neared the cave, a familiar sensation swept over her – the same one she'd felt in the graveyard when she knew the ghost was near.

The ghost who'd kidnapped the moose all those years ago. *Before* he was a ghost.

Thatch felt it, too. Up ahead, he slowed. When Beka saw the hair on his back ruffle, warning bells rang in her brain.

Was the moose-napper waiting for them to enter the dark cave?

Was this a trick?

"Raz, wait." Catching up with Robbie, she grabbed his arm.

"Are you feeling the same thing I'm

feeling?" he asked.

She nodded, amazed she didn't need to explain her sudden fear.

Robbie watched her face. "Do you think it's—?"

"Yes," Beka whispered. "I think we have company."

"But doesn't he *want* us to find the moose? To clear his conscience?"

Find what's missing; never mind the thief echoed through Beka's mind. "Yes, he wants the moose found. He showed us the final clue that brought us here."

She paused. "I hate to say this, but he *might* be getting a kick out of scaring us."

Robbie sniggered. "You hate to say it because that's what *you* do – scare people just for fun."

Beka gave him a guilty look. He was right. The graveyard ghost was giving her a taste of her own medicine.

Meanwhile, Jamie had reached the rocks, and was scouting for the entrance.

"We can't let her go in alone," Robbie said.

He raced ahead, leaving Beka behind.

"How do you plan to stop her?" she yelled, running to catch up.

Jamie stopped to examine some overgrown bushes.

"These can't be huckleberries," she said. "I don't see berries on the branches at all. Maybe I'm in the wrong place."

"No, you're not," Beka told her. "Those are huckleberry bushes just starting to flower. The berries won't show up until summer."

Robbie nodded his agreement.

Still, Jamie looked unsure. "It's cold here," she whispered, rubbing her arms. "Much colder than the meadow."

Beka had also sensed the drop in temperature as they neared the cave. "Ghost chill," she explained. "You're surrounded by four of us."

Thatch finished sniffing the area, then disappeared into the underbrush.

Beka followed, figuring the dog knew where to look better than she could guess.

He led her to a low rounded rock. The

middle was hollowed out, exposing a black, yawning hole.

"Thatch found it!" Beka shouted.

Robbie caught up, rewarding Thatch with a belly rub.

The twins waited until Jamie worked her way around the rocks. "Here it is," she whispered, bending to keep from banging her head on the low entrance.

Inside, she paused, groaning, "Why didn't I bring a torch? I knew I was looking for a cave."

"Can't help you there," Beka said. "Sorry."

Stepping out into the sunshine, Jamie blinked. "I don't have *time* to go after a torch," she argued with herself. "If the moose is in here, it should be big enough to find by touch."

"By touch?" Robbie echoed.

"If Gran can see with her fingers, so can I." Heaving a determined sigh, Jamie stooped and entered the cave, holding one arm to the side to feel her way along the wall. The other, she swooped back and forth in front of her, the way Gran swooped her cane.

The last thing Beka wanted to do was follow.

Not Thatch. Her noble dog. He was right on Jamie's heels.

Only he was trying to take hold of her shirt to tug her back. To tug her *out* of the cave.

Thatch knew they weren't alone. Whether or not the ghost was toying with them didn't matter to the dog. He was simply doing his job.

Robbie stepped into the cave.

"Wait!" Beka called.

"What, Sis? We *have* to go with her."

"Even if *he's* in there?"

Robbie looked as determined as Jamie. "He can't hurt me."

The twins already knew rules of the ghost world weren't the same as the "real world". Maybe the ghost wanted *Jamie* to find the moose. All by herself. Maybe he wanted *other* ghosts – meaning them – to get lost. "Raz, you don't *know* whether or not he can hurt you."

"Be-ka." Giving her an exasperated look,

Robbie turned and entered the cave. In three steps, darkness swallowed him.

She kicked at the rock, wishing she was home, safe in her attic. "Well," she announced to the berry-less bushes. "I am *not* a coward. If Jamie can find her way through the cave by touch, so can I."

With one glance behind at the comforting blue sky, Beka headed inside, stumbling over rocks in the cold, dark cave – knowing she was hurrying straight towards the terrifying *whatever* that had chased her away from the graveyard.

Chapter 19
For Ghost Ears Only

The tunnel twisted and turned, cutting off daylight.

If that alone wasn't enough to scare anyone, Thatch's constant growling was guaranteed to finish the job.

The big question was: Could the growling scare off another ghost?

Up ahead came the sound of Jamie's laughter, floating in the darkness to Beka's ears.

How can she laugh at a time like this?

Beka trudged forward. With each step, the presence of the ghost grew stronger. The feeling was eerie and foreboding.

Yet, it wasn't one of *danger*. Danger is what she'd felt in the cemetery.

This feeling was heavy and suffocating – more a sense of another presence, watching and waiting.

Yes. Beka remembered. The sensation in the cemetery had been one of warning. This was different.

Intrigued, she quickened her steps, tripping on rocks in the dark.

"Sis," came Robbie's voice, "give me your hand."

Beka moved ahead until she found him. Blindly, she reached out, unsure where Robbie was or what he planned to do.

Taking her hand, he placed it against something cold, hard, and too smooth to be the wall of the cave.

"Is this it?" Beka yelped. "Is this the moose?" Suddenly Jamie's laughter made sense.

The sensation of not being able to see, even with eyes wide open was strange, yet when Beka ran her hand over the long snout, the antlers, the high flank, she felt like she was greeting an old friend.

Her fingers "told" her the form was dusty. Her nose told her it was mouldy. Yet it was definitely the shape of what they'd been searching for.

Beka's anxiety melted into excitement.

They'd found the missing moose!

As the group felt its way back to the entrance, the hair on Beka's arms suddenly began to tingle, shoving her into a run.

"*Woof!*" Thatch brought up the rear, urging the other two into a run as well, almost as if he was herding them out of the cave.

Slipping and sliding on loose rocks, terror streaked through Beka as she stumbled her way outside with the others.

Panting, Jamie leaned against the rock. "What?" she gasped. "What happened?"

"Something spooked us," Robbie said, tensed, as if he was ready to keep running. "Ah," he glanced at Beka. "The moose-napper?"

She nodded, unable to tear her attention

away from the entrance to the cave.

Robbie seemed confused. "But, I thought he *wanted* us to find this place. Maybe he *doesn't* want the moose removed?"

As if in answer, a frigid gust of wind blasted their faces, almost bowling them over.

Jamie grasped the rock to steady herself.

On the wings of the breeze came a willowy voice, rising into the air and floating away.

The words "Th-h-h-a-a-a-n-k yo-o-o-u-u-u-u…" mingled among the sounds of the forest so faintly, only a ghost's ears could have heard… And understood.

Chapter 20
Morty, Good as New

The instant Jamie stepped into the *Makanda Room*, Mr Tavolott rushed to her side.

"Go tell your grandmother you're back," he urged. "Nell's been beside herself, wondering why your errand took so long."

He put a hand on Jamie's shoulder, waiting for her to catch her breath. "Are you all right, young lady?"

Jamie nodded. "Yes, but it's *you* I need to talk to."

"Me?" Mr Tavolott looked surprised, then concerned. "Is something wrong?"

"Not any more," Jamie said, laughing. "I

found the moose!"

Mr Tavolott cocked his head, confused. "*What* moose?"

"Juniper's missing moose. From the town square."

The mayor had to steady himself against the wall. His eyes registered disbelief and hope at the same time.

"It's in a cave near Danger Cove," Jamie told him. "I couldn't bring it back by myself."

Mr Tavolott's laughter boomed across the room, making visitors at the showing stop and smile in his direction. "Morty weighs over four hundred pounds. Of course you couldn't bring him back by yourself."

Acting delighted, he quickly gathered a few strong volunteers in the alley. Jamie gave directions. In minutes, the men were off on their quest.

"Our moose!" Mr Tavolott hugged Jamie. "How can I ever thank you?"

She shrugged. "I just want to see it before I leave. That's all."

Robbie raced back to Beka after watching

the volunteers leave. "Do you want to follow them to rescue the moose?" he asked, looking hopeful.

She shook her head. "No thank you. One cave a day is my limit."

Jamie trotted across the room to tell her grandmother the news, but a line of admirers kept her from Gran. Giving up, she stationed herself by the alley door to wait for the "rescuers" to return.

The twins drifted towards the buffet table. When no one was looking, they pinched brownies for themselves, and for Thatch, of course. He'd never allow them to have a treat and not include him.

Finally Gran broke away from the crowd, depending on a librarian to lead her to Jamie.

The twins trotted over so they could listen to Jamie's version of the story.

"Your father will be proud of your sleuthing," Gran said, giving her a hug. "You solved the mystery – and in the nick of time," she added. "Run and tell Charles we're ready to go."

"Oh, Grandma Nell." Jamie clasped her hands together to beg. "Can't we stay a little longer? I never got to *see* the moose, only touch him."

Her grandmother's face turned misty. "I can relate to that," she said, reaching out to her granddaughter. "I'm sorry, child, but we can't miss our flight. We have to get home and pack for Italy – and humour Bartholomew and Dr Tekoa."

Turning, she asked the librarian to check her watch, then added, "Another fifteen minutes is all we can spare."

Robbie paced with Jamie. For fifteen minutes.

Finally Gran bade goodbye to everyone, after agreeing to leave her paintings on display for two weeks so everyone in Juniper would have a chance to see them.

Mr Tavolott escorted Gran to the alley, where the limo still waited – this time to take her and Jamie to the airport.

He helped her into the front seat, then opened the back door for Jamie.

"What's this?" Jamie scooped a small bouquet of wild flowers off the seat. Flowers from the meadow at Danger Cove.

"Ewww," Beka teased, nudging her blushing brother. "Nice touch."

"Glory be!" Mr Tavolott exclaimed. "Looks as though Miss Jamie has a secret admirer."

Jamie touched the flowers to her cheek, giggling. "I never saw any boys here – except the one in the painting." She froze as her words reminded her what *happened* to the boy in the painting.

Beka thought it was hysterical. "She's thinking about you," she purred.

"I know," Robbie snapped. Still he couldn't hide his grin.

Jamie's gaze flitted about the alley, almost as if she expected to see the boy standing among the crowd. "Thank you," she whispered, but only the ghost twins could hear.

"Gosh, it was nothing," Robbie mumbled.

A horn blast drew everyone's attention.

Up chugged a pickup truck. In its bed

stood a mouldy, dusty, and generally pitiful-looking moose.

Mr Tavolott quickly described the scene to Gran.

"A gallon of my turpentine ought to clean up Morty as good as new," she said. "And it sounds like my granddaughter *might* become a detective instead of an artist. Who knows?"

A cheer burst from the crowd. Someone shouted, "Let's hear it for Jamie Makanda, rescuer of our missing moose!"

"With a little help from the ghost twins," Beka singsonged.

"Woof, woof!"

"Oh, yeah," she laughed. "And our moose-hunting ghost dog, too."

Author's Note

Grandma Nell's canaries, Picasso and Dalí, are named after two "modern" artists, Pablo Picasso and Salvador Dalí.

Picasso is the most famous painter of our century. He became known for his sculpture, drawings, and ceramics as well. Picasso started painting when he was only 14 years old. Many of his people and animals are shown with their eyes at odd angles, or out of place. (Pablo Picasso [Pih-KASS-oh] 1881–1973, Spanish)

Dalí is easily recognized by his swirly moustache. His pictures combine unusual objects with realistic figures. They look like something you might see in one of your craziest dreams. He even called his work "hand-painted dream photographs". This type of art is "surrealism". (Salvador Dalí [DAH-lee] 1904–1989, Spanish)

Here are the other artists
Gran and Jamie mention:

Delacroix – His paintings were inspired by the writings of Shakespeare and other famous authors including Dante, Lord Byron, and Sir Walter Scott. His fellow painters didn't care for his work because he didn't follow tradition. Yet he is seen as the forerunner of modern art. (Eugene Delacroix [DELL-a-croy] 1798–1863, French)

Monet – He liked to paint outdoor scenes, quickly, based on his own response to the setting. This practice became known as "impressionist" painting. Sometimes he painted the same scene over and over to show the changing light as the sun moved across the sky. (Claude Monet [MON-ay] 1840–1926, French)

Van Gogh – He is one of the most famous artists of all time, yet while he lived, he sold only one painting and considered himself a complete failure. During the last five years of his life, he completed more than 800 paintings. Van Gogh believed himself mad (he even cut off his own ear!). He took his own life at the age of thirty-seven. (Vincent Van Gogh [Van-GO] 1853–1890, Dutch)

Botticelli – He is best known for his illustrations of Dante's *Divine Comedy*, and his many religious paintings, especially of the Madonna. He once heard a preacher warn of "worldliness", and was so moved, he burned all of his paintings that were *not* religious. (Sandro Botticelli [Bot-a-CHELL-ee] about 1444–1510, Italian)

Cassatt – She became known for her peaceful paintings of children with their mothers, and liked to draw ordinary people doing ordinary things. She was born in Pennsylvania, but spent many years living in France, where other artists, like her friend Edgar Degas lived. (Mary Cassatt [Ka-SAT] 1844–1926, American)

Matisse – He was leader of the *"fauves"*, a group of painters who worked with bright colours, bold patterns, and quick brush strokes. Their style shocked the Paris art world of the early 1900s. In French, the word *fauve* means "wild beast". (Henri Matisse [Mah-TEESE] 1869–1954, French)

Degas – He liked to show people in unposed, natural scenes, catching them in "private moments". He travelled to Italy to study the great painters in history in order to perfect his own style. He was also influenced by Japanese art to use "daring" angles and odd viewpoints, while still maintaining balance in his paintings. (Edgar Degas [DAY-gar] 1834–1917, French)

Rules to be Ghosts by…

1. Ghosts can touch objects, but not people or animals. Our hands go right through them.
2. Ghosts can cause "a disturbance" around people to get their attention. Here are three ways: walk through them; yell and scream a lot; chant a message over and over.
3. Rules of the world don't apply to ghosts.
4. Thatch's ghost-dog powers are stronger than ours. He can do things we can't. Sometimes he even teaches us things we didn't know we could do.
5. Ghosts can't move through closed doors,

walls, or windows (but we can *smoosh* through if there is one tiny hole).

6. Ghosts don't need to eat, but they can if they want to.

7. Ghosts can listen in on other people's conversations.

8. Ghosts can move objects by concentrating on them until they move into the other dimension and become invisible. When we let go of the object, it becomes visible again.

9. Ghosts don't need to sleep, but can rest by "floating". If our energy is drained (by too much haunting or *smooshing*) we must return to Kickingbird Lake to renew our strength.

10. Ghosts can move from one place to another by thinking hard about where we want to be, and wishing it. All three of us must be touching to make it work.